The Crone's Curse

A Willows Bend Cozy Mystery- Book 2

Evelyn Cullet

Amazon KDP

Published by Evelyn Cullet

Typesetting services by BOOKOW.COM

To my niece, Cathy Tervanis. Thanks for your good wishes and continued support. You have no idea how much they mean to me. Love ya!

Acknowledgments

Book Cover Designed by: Margarita Felix of 100 Covers
Editor: Erynn Newman, A Little Red Ink.

Chapter 1

HEATHER Stanton awoke to a loud thump. She blinked into the darkness of the hotel room she'd been sharing with her aunt. Was someone trying to break in?

Heart pounding, she sat up in bed, her mouth so dry she could barely swallow.

Another *Thump... clunk...* Then... a woman's quiet groan.

She gasped, and with a trembling hand, switched on the nightstand light.

Kneeling by the modest closet, her aunt tossed out shoes as if they were trash. Heather got out of bed, grabbed the water bottle from the night stand, and walked over to her.

"You scared me. What are you doing?"

Julia glanced up. "I have to find my red stilettos."

"In the dark?" Heather swigged the water as she checked the time on the bedside clock. "At three in the morning?"

Julia waved a hand at her. "Don't bother me. I have to find those shoes."

What's wrong with my aunt's memory? "You pawned them last week because you said they were killing your feet."

"Don't be silly. I wouldn't get rid of those shoes. I can't go to the Belmont Stakes race in my bedroom slippers, can I?"

Aunt Julia and horses. Will she ever stop betting on the races? Heather gripped her aunt's arm to help her stand.

"You can't leave town for the next few months, until the end of your community service sentence, so the Belmont Stakes is out. The only place you're going is back to sleep."

Julia's thin, graying eyebrows scrunched as she ambled to her bed. "Promise you'll help me find those shoes?"

"I promise."

Heather climbed into her own bed, slid under the covers, and turned off the light. Her eyelids closed as thoughts of her aunt played in her mind. Julia had done some odd things in the past, but this behavior was crazy, even for her.

Maybe the trauma she suffered from finding a dead man, and being a suspect in his murder, had now manifested in sleepwalking. Her aunt should have talked to a counselor at the time, like the police suggested, but she refused. Too stubborn.

Now that their lives had gone back to relative normalcy, Julia seemed like her old self. *Maybe sleepwalking will be a one-time thing.*

***

In the morning, Heather dropped her aunt off at Willows Park for her second day of community service and drove back to the Franklin House Hotel. Breakfast was compli mentary, so she decided to take advantage.

Grabbing a copy of the local paper from the front counter, she waved hello to Vikki Garrett, the twenty-something desk clerk, and headed to the breakfast room.

She loaded her plate with eggs, bacon, and toast, and made her way to a table in the corner near a small television. The weather lady on the local news station predicted today would be warm and sunny. Typical weather for May, and perfect for what she had to do. Opening the newspaper, she searched the ads for furnished apartments for rent.

Heather circled the two offered units and finished her toast. Making a life-changing decision usually killed her appetite, but deciding to stay in Willows Bend with her aunt was what she needed right now, a change from her previous manic job as a Marketing Account Executive in Chicago.

The breakfast room buzzed with other guests coming and going. She wrapped her hands around her coffee mug and drew in its strong scent. Her feet itched to be up and running. She wasn't being lazy—this was small-town living. Time to get used to it.

A tall, dark-haired man approached her table from the lobby. She leaned forward, admiring his easy, confident walk and the way his muscles moved under his sports shirt. With his sky-blue eyes, Chad Willows looked as scrumptious as her breakfast had tasted. Hard to believe she already had warm feelings for the ex-P.I. turned bookstore owner. It had only been a week since they'd teamed up to clear her aunt of an impending murder charge.

But this wasn't the time to consider starting a new relationship. She'd recently ended a long one with a womanizing divorce lawyer.

She stood to greet Chad. "Hi, what are you doing here?"

"I dropped off a couple of books the desk clerk ordered. We're closing the store early for inventory, so she wouldn't be able to pick them up today. As I was passing, I noticed you sitting here engrossed in our local newspaper. If you don't mind my asking, what could you possibly find so fascinating in this little town? Nothing much ever happens here."

Heather picked up the paper. "I've been searching the ads for an apartment to rent, but there are only two that are furnished."

"I might be able to help you. Let me see the paper." He shook his head as he read the ads. "The one at the top of the page is okay but pricy. The other's in a rundown part of town, not sure you'd want to live there."

"That's the way my luck's been running these days. Where do you suggest I look now? We can't stay at this hotel much longer. It's costing us a fortune."

He hesitated a moment as the corner of his lips lifted in a half-smile. "I might have the perfect place for you and your aunt."

This sounded like it could be a sure thing. "As long as it's not too expensive. We're on limited budgets."

Chad slipped a hand into his pants pocket and pulled out a set of keys on a silver ring. "I'm sure we can work something out. But I have to warn you, the place isn't big."

"Anything larger than a hotel room is acceptable to me, and I'm sure my aunt will agree."

Chad checked his cell phone. "I've got some time now. Would you like to see it?"

"I'm free." She hoped he'd take the words literally.

She grabbed her purse as a special report flashed across the television screen. A view of Willows Park came up. Her Aunt Julia stood near the rose garden talking to a short, balding man in a beige suit, whom Heather recognized as Homicide Detective Ben Lindsey, from their encounter last week. In the background, uniformed police officers cordoned off the area.

Chad motioned toward the screen. "Isn't that your aunt?"

Heather's jaw dropped as her stomach clenched.

The voice of the local news anchor announced, "The body of an elderly woman was discovered in the garden area at Willows Park this morning by community service worker, Julia Fairchild. The dead woman's name is being withheld pending next of kin notification. We'll report more details as they become available."

"Oh, my God!" Heather pulled out her cell phone and tapped the screen, but the call to her aunt was picked up by voice mail. She left a message. "I saw the awful news on TV. Call me as soon as you can."

Heather grabbed her car keys. "I have to get down there. My aunt might need me."

Chad rubbed his clean-shaven jaw. "From what I've seen of her, I'm pretty sure she can take care of herself."

"Usually, I'd agree with you, but she hasn't been herself, lately." *At least she wasn't last night.*

Chapter 2

Heather sped through two yellow lights, racing to reach Willows Park. *What has my aunt gotten herself into now?* She pulled up to the curb, got out, and double-stepped it along the lagoon to reach the flower garden.

Huffing for breath, Heather approached Officer Henderson, who, with several other uniformed police, held off the crowd of townspeople, mostly elderly, trying to get through to see what the fuss was about.

Heather glanced up at the officer's tanned face. "Hi. Do you remember me?"

"How could I forget? Your aunt is *so delightful to be around.*" The sarcastic tone of his voice was undeniable.

Julia's snide remarks about how the police in this town had treated her when she was in custody last week must have ticked him off.

"I need to see her." Heather pointed. "Over there by the rose garden."

"Sorry, no one goes near the area until Detective Lindsey says so. You'll have to wait here like everyone else."

Heather placed her fists on her hips in her most intimidating stance. "How long will that take?"

"As long as it takes." The officer leaned in closer. "Here's a little advice. The detective will be taking your aunt to the station to make an official statement some time this morning, so why don't you wait for her to call you."

Easy for you to say. "Can you at least tell me who the dead woman is?"

"Sorry, no."

Heather trudged back to her rental car and drove to the *Willow in the Wind* bookstore owned by Chad Willows and his younger sister, Ashley.

Chad stood outside the store staring at the cell phone in his hand, his dark, neatly trimmed, hair nearly touching the forest green awning he stood under. As she approached, he slipped the phone into his pants pocket. "Is your aunt all right? What did you find out?"

Heather let out a breath of frustration. "The police are so infuriating. They won't let me talk to her, and they won't tell me who the dead woman is. I'll have to wait until the news is released, or she comes back from her interview at the station. Since there isn't anything I can do for her right now, I wouldn't mind seeing the apartment you said was available."

"You're here." He pointed upward. "It's on the second floor, but the outside entrance is around the corner."

Chad unlocked the side door, and they walked up the narrow stairs in silence. At the top, he slipped the key into the lock. "You'll have to do some cleaning up. My sister was going to refurbished the place after our granddad passed away, and she got as far as emptying out most of his things, which she had someone put in the attic, but now..."

Since he'd left the sentence hanging, Heather grabbed the opportunity to finally ask why his younger sister was in a wheelchair—something she'd been putting off because she didn't want to seem nosy.

"What happened to Ashley?"

"Hit and run."

"Did the police catch the driver?"

"No. Or I should say, not yet."

"She's such a lovely person. How severe are her injuries?"

"There's always hope, and Ashley's determined to walk again. Of course, her dreams of becoming an Olympic swimmer are crushed. This was her last year to qualify."

Heather couldn't find the right words to express her concern. She never could. But if she didn't say anything, she'd appear cold and heartless, a reputation she'd gotten in the past from friends and family.

"I'm so sorry." It was a pretty standard statement, but the best she could do at the moment.

Chad nodded his acknowledgement. He pushed the door open and pulled the thick, gold, living room drapes aside.

Heather walked into the compact apartment and gazed at the rows of books lining one of the walls. Hard covers and paperbacks filled every inch of space on the dark pine shelves.

"Sorry, I had to leave Granddad's books up here. There's no room in the store right now, but I'll get them out of your way as soon as I can."

"You don't have to. I like them. They add a certain ambiance to the room."

The opposite wall held a wood-burning fireplace that had seen its share of use judging from the blackened grate.

Heather strolled over to the gold-brocade sofa. "What style of furniture is this?"

"Open Hearth. It was popular when my grandfather furnished the place in the seventies."

No knickknacks or frilly lace adorned the dark pine end tables. Definitely a man's apartment.

She followed Chad down a short hall. "There's a galley kitchen, two bedrooms, a bathroom, and a small utility room with a compact washer-dryer. My granddad often had stay-over guests."

Heather could imagine them sitting in front of an open fire, discussing rare books while sipping an exceptional fifty-year-old brandy.

The apartment was a stroke of luck. But she had one concern.

"Aren't you a little uncomfortable with us here in your granddad's home with his furniture and all your memories of him?"

Chad cleared his throat. "I'm sorry if I misled you. This was his place for out-of-town friends to stay, or if he wanted to entertain guests privately. Sometimes, if he worked late, he'd sleep here, but he didn't live here. It's okay if you'd rather move your own furniture and things in."

"My aunt's been traveling, and I moved into my former boyfriend's condo right from my family's home, so neither of us have anything to move in. That's why we need a furnished apartment. But we're not staying permanently, only for the time my aunt's serving her community service sentence. So if we can rent it on a monthly basis, this will be perfect."

Chad handed her the keys. "It's yours. But you should have your aunt see the apartment before you make a final decision."

"You're right. I'll bring her by after she finishes for the day, or with the police, whichever comes first."

Heather's cell rang. She checked the caller ID and gave a mental groan. *Mom.*

"Excuse me. I should take this."

"I have to go anyway. Talk to you later." Chad swung the door closed behind him.

Heather stared at her cell phone and gritted her teeth.

If she hadn't run into her Aunt Julia in this small town right after her life had fallen apart, she would probably have ended up moving back into her mother's house, hiding out in her old room, having to endure repetitive lectures on her numerous failings. *Why can't you be like your sister, Emily, the married, assistant college professor?*

She closed her eyes a moment to gather her courage and answered the call. "Hi Mom. How was your church-group trip?"

"The Michigan wine country was great. But never mind me. When I got back, I listened to a voice-mail message from my sister giving me a short rundown of what happened to you both while I was away. Why didn't you call me?"

Heather cringed at the thought of telling her mother about her aunt being suspected of murder.

"I didn't want to ruin your trip."

"It wouldn't have been the first time Julia has ruined things for me." Her mom sucked in a breath. "Where is *Willows Bend* anyway?"

"It's a lovely little town about half-way between Chicago and Champaign."

"I've repeatedly warned you about your temper. And now look where it's gotten you—out on your ear and living in *no man's land* with that horse-playing sister of mine who doesn't know the meaning of responsibility. Come home, and let me help you."

Didn't her mother realize if she wanted to go home, she would have? She had no problem controlling her temper, although it had led to her meltdown and rage-quitting her stressful job in Chicago, then storming out on her unfaithful boyfriend.

"Are you listening to me? "Unconsciously, Heather had tuned her mother out. Mrs. Stanton gave one of her long-suffering sighs. "When are you coming home? If you don't, you'll end up aimlessly wandering the streets like your aunt."

At this point in the conversation, Heather wanted to bang her head against the kitchen wall. She wasn't anything like her free-wheeling aunt. But then, her mother was always making comparisons.

"And what about your job? How are you planning to support yourself now?"

There was always the possibility of turning her knack for marketing into an online career. She'd done it in college to make a little spending money, but that small amount of business was a long way from being able to support herself.

"I'm exploring a few things. I'll manage." She pushed away a twinge of uncertainty.

"While you're living with your aunt, promise you'll keep a close eye on her. Julia's already gotten you into trouble once. What's to say it won't happen again?"

Heather dreaded having to tell her mother her aunt had found another dead body. So she didn't. "I'm sure Aunt Julia will be good while she's here."

"Don't say I didn't warn you."

There was a strained pause while Heather's ears burned with irritation. "You should be grateful to your sister. She was the only person who came to help when you had your breakdown after dad deserted us." *It was fortunate too, because I couldn't have handled you on my own while Emily was away at college.*

"That's the problem with your aunt. One minute she's there for you, all caring and supportive, and the next... she's gone."

"She can't run this time, Mom, not until she finishes her community service sentence."

"Or until she gets bored."

Heather grabbed this opportunity to end the call. "I'll email you with our new address. Bye."

She tossed the phone on the counter.

Would there ever be a time when her mother didn't make her crazy?

Chapter 3

THAT afternoon, Heather drove to the park to pick up her aunt, who was waiting near the still cordoned-off rose garden. As she approached, she found Julia talking on her cell. Heather's gaze met hers.

"I'll call you back." Her aunt slipped the phone into her pants pocket.

Heather couldn't help but hug her. "Oh, Aunt Julia. I was so worried. What happened here this morning?"

"Didn't you catch the news? Those annoying reporters were poking their noses into every detail."

"I saw some of it, but I'd like to hear the rest from you."

"There." Julia pointed to part of the garden near a wrought-iron bench. That's where I was going to plant those petunias." She moved her finger to the side, indicating the tray of flowers on the ground. "Guess I dug the bed a little too deep, because a body was under the fresh dirt the garden center had dumped yesterday. I thought someone had buried a piece of clothing, until I noticed the gray hair. And then I saw the..." She sucked in a breath and swallowed hard. "Face."

"Did you tell your supervisor?"

"There isn't one. Officer Henderson comes by a few times a day to check up on me. I didn't get his cell number, so I called Detective Lindsey." Julia bent her head down and kicked at the grass near the wrought-iron bench. "He grilled me about it like he thought I did it." She crossed her arms.

Heather could easily imagine what the detective said to her aunt. This was the second dead body Julia found in a week. "What happened then?"

"He took me to the station to make a statement and finally drove me here to finish out the day. As if I felt like coming back to the scene of the crime." Julia lowered herself onto the wrought-iron bench and popped a tiny mint into her mouth, her version of Xanax.

"At least you didn't know the victim this time."

"Well... I didn't 'actually' know her."

Uh, oh. "What do you mean by *actually?*"

Julia pursed her lips and gazed skyward as if she expected the answer to drop down from above. Then she let out a sorrowful-sounding sigh. "When you and I delivered those flowers you wanted to get rid of, to the retirement village, a few days ago. I liked the place, so while you spoke with the managing director, I questioned some of the residents."

"I wondered where you'd disappeared to."

"One of the residents was a cranky senior, Esther Kwinn. She's the woman I found... dead. I recognized the same ugly, purple and green crocheted vest she had on when I spoke to her."

"Go on."

"Anyway," Julia continued. "We discussed certain... *things.*"

A note of angst flitted across Heather's heart. Whenever her aunt hesitated and then said the word, "things," it meant she was holding something back.

"What things?"

"We kind of had an argument."

"How do you *kind of* have an argument?"

Julia ran a hand through her mess of bright auburn hair, making an already wild look, even wilder. It was her way of stalling.

"Esther called me some nasty names because I was involved in the murder last week. So I came back at her with a raised voice. She got in my face and said they didn't need my kind in this town. I might have pushed her a little, to get her out of my way, and I left." Julia rose to her feet and popped another peppermint into her mouth. "But there was one tiny problem."

Why is it with my aunt, there's always a problem? Heather caught her breath in mock surprise. "Only one?"

"Don't get snarky with me. I had enough from Lindsey."

Aunt Julia had always been a tough cookie on the outside, but inside, not so much.

"You're right. I'm sorry. Finish your story."

"Some people heard us. And now Detective Lindsey considers me a person of interest in this murder case."

Heather closed her eyes and tried not to think about it. Another murder was more than she could handle right now.

"But I swear to you, I didn't kill Esther. Honestly."

Heather patted her aunt's slumping shoulder. "You don't have to convince me. I believe you."

How does Aunt Julia get herself into these things?

"I have some positive news." Heather smiled. A change of subject was something they could both use right about then. "Chad Willows showed me the most adorable apartment this morning, right above the book-store. We can rent it on a monthly basis. And it's even furnished."

Julia said a less than enthusiastic, "Oh?"

"Don't make a judgment about it until you've seen the place. It's small but quaint. And Chad told me the rent will be reasonable."

"I'm not judging. It's probably charming."

"We can get Chinese take-out for dinner and then go to the apartment. If you like the place, Chad said we can move in tomorrow morning. We have to check out of the hotel by eleven, or they'll charge us for another day."

"If you like the apartment, I'm sure I will too."

Why was her aunt being so agreeable? This wasn't like her. She was usually critical of everything. Maybe it was the trauma of finding another dead body. Or maybe she found out something at the police station and concocted a crazy scheme to investigate the death of Ester Kwinn on her own.

Chapter 4

A T the apartment, Heather walked behind her aunt as Julia inspected all the rooms.

"Do you like it?"

"I approve."

"Great. Let's go down to the bookstore. We need to sign our renters' agreement and give Chad the deposit." Heather headed toward the door.

"Wait," Julia said. "I'll write you a check for my half of the rent. How much is it?" She plopped onto the sofa and opened her purse.

"I was so excited about getting the apartment, I forgot to ask. But Chad said we could work something out, payment-wise."

Julia closed her purse and sighed.

"What's wrong? Have you changed your mind?"

"No, it doesn't have anything to do with the apartment. I can't help thinking about the murder. I don't understand why these horrible things keep happening to me. I've tried to live an exemplary life."

As a young woman, Julia had all the advantages, intelligence, beauty, a college education, but she got mixed up with some bad men, and then she became addicted to gambling on horse racing—although Julia had never considered it an addiction to racing, more like a predilection for horses.

A few moments later, Julia sucked in a deep breath. "The only explanation I have for these horrible things happening to me is... the *crone's curse!*"

Her aunt often had crazy ideas, but this was one of the worst. "What are you talking about?"

"Before I got stuck in this town, I was involved with a man in Chicago who'd recently arrived in the States from Hungary."

I'm not surprised. Most of Aunt Julia's trouble starts with a man.

Julia gazed upward to recall the incident. "He was charming, with old world manners and a bright smile. He seemed to be genuinely into me. At the time, I needed someone like him to lean on for understanding and support. But things were moving too fast. Something wasn't right."

Julia clenched a fist at her stomach. "I could feel it in my gut. Then I overheard people talking about him and found out he would marry any woman to stay in this country. Of course, I dumped him. Not only because I didn't want to be tied down to a man who didn't love me, but I also didn't want to pay a $250,000 fine and spend five years in prison if the I.N.S. found out."

"I don't blame you."

Julia raised her palms in the air. "How could I have guessed his crone of a mother would put a curse on me. I swear she came out of nowhere, and she looked like Maria Ouspenskaya from the old movie, *The Wolfman.* Same face, same voice, same everything."

Aunt Julia and her references to old movies—Heather wasn't familiar with most of them, and she hadn't seen his one. "You shouldn't call his mother a crone."

"Well, she was, and you can't tell me different. I know a crone when I see one." Julia wiggled her fingers around her face in a frantic gesture, obviously to make a point. "They've all got those penetrating, deep-set eyes, the dangling earrings, the wrinkled skin, and those facial warts." She shuddered. "And now..." She glanced from side to side. "*The curse* is coming true."

How can she believe such nonsense? "What did this woman say to make you think she's put a curse on you?"

Julia hesitated a moment. "Let's see if I can recall the words. *'See the pain you have caused my son with your cruelty. I move my finger three times three.'* And she did, right in my face. Then she said, *'when the light fades and darkness comes through, the shrouds of misfortune and death will burden you.'* Then she added, *'to the end of your days.'"*

Heather stopped herself from rolling her eyes. "That's kind of vague. What's it supposed to mean?"

"It means death is following me, and dreadful things are always going to happen. And they already have. Death *has* followed me... twice." Julia gasped. "I almost forgot to tell you the most important part. To top it off, as if to set the whole thing in motion, she spit on my shoes."

Heather coughed to suppress a laugh. "They wouldn't happen to have been those red stiletto sandals you once owned?"

"How did you know?"

"A good guess. You were searching for them at three this morning. In the dark."

"Why would I do that? I pawned those shoes last week. I don't need a reminder of the curse. You must have been dreaming."

"It wasn't a dream. You were sleepwalking."

Julia opened her mouth and then closed it again. "I've never sleepwalked in my life." She touched her full lips as her large brown eyes widened. "Maybe it's part of the curse."

Heather could only think of one thing to say. "There's no such thing as a curse. They're only words, and if you choose not to believe them, they won't affect you."

"Bite your tongue!" Julia raised a finger. "*There are more things in Heaven and Earth, Horatio...*"

Now she's quoting Shakespeare. "I understand what you're saying. Yes, someone else has died. But it's only a matter of you being in the wrong place at the wrong time. Only a coincidence."

Julia's lightly penciled-in eyebrows lowered in a look that said she wasn't convinced.

Chapter 5

JULIA had slept through the night without waking or walking, as far as Heather was aware.

In the morning, they got up early, packed their luggage and took it to the cozy new apartment. Then Heather dropped her aunt off at the park and drove to the supermarket to stock up on groceries.

Back at the apartment, she opened her Chanel Duffle Keepall and pulled out the laptop. In a few moments, her new marketing website came up. She admired the sharply crafted design, a combination of her own ideas and a few of her sister's, whom she'd called for advice. She'd made all the arrangements to set herself up as a company and contacted her former clients to notify them she was out on her own. Now she accessed her "Contact Me" page, anxious to see the results.

"Nothing yet?" She tapped her nails on the table as her shoulders dropped. *Darn.* "Maybe a boost of caffeine will make me feel better about the marketing sector ignoring me."

She strode to the kitchen to pour herself a fresh cup of coffee. Murmurs sounded from her bedroom, like people were in there talking. But she was the only one in the apartment.

"Must be a clock radio."

She went to turn it off. But there wasn't one in the room. The murmurs sounded louder. She glanced around and listened. Voices drifted up through the floor vent. She had to be standing over the back room of the bookstore.

Heather knelt and reached for the lever to close it but hesitated. It wasn't ethical to eavesdrop. And sometimes she'd heard things she'd wished she hadn't. But the urge was overwhelming. *Maybe this once.*

It was hard to make out the murmurings, so she scrunched down and put her ear to the vent.

"Come on, Chad. I can read you like an open book. You like her," Ashley said.

Makki meowed. Heather could imagine the adorable black cat with the large, green eyes sitting on Ashley's lap.

The sound of a chair scraped across the floor. "What's not to like? She's intelligent, witty, gorgeous. Not to mention having a great body."

Could he be talking about me? Warmth rushed to Heather's cheeks. She wasn't sure if it was from Chad's comment or from having her face so close to the heating vent.

"Why don't you ask her out?" Ashley asked.

Heather held her breath, waiting for Chad's answer.

"I would if it wasn't for the fact that she..."

Yeow! Makki screeched.

That darn cat

A door opened. "Grab him," Ashley said. And then silence.

Heather shut the vent and sagged against the wall. "The fact that I'm what?" She wasn't perfect, so it could me any number of things. Of course, they might've been talking about some other woman in town, including Chad's ex. *Wish I hadn't listened. Thinking about this is going to drive me to distraction.*

An urgent banging on the living room door startled her. *Who could that be?*

"I'm coming."

Heather smoothed her wrinkled clothes as she made her way to the door. It couldn't be her aunt, and not many people knew she'd moved in here. She hadn't even gone to the post office to change her address yet.

Opening the door, a gray-haired man sporting two-day-old whiskers stumbled his way into the living room.

Heather sucked in a breath. *The nerve.* "Who are you? What do you want?"

"Where's Willows?" The demand rode in on a wave of stale tobacco smoke.

She left the door open, in case she had to run down the stairs in a hurry. "From what I understand, Mr. Willows passed away about three months ago. I live here now."

His cracked lips scrunched into a frown as he pulled a cigarette from the pocket of his brown bomber jacket. "If Willows's dead, how come his furniture and stuff's still around, like it was the last time I was here?"

"I rented the apartment already furnished." She'd better say something that sounded as intimidating as he appeared. "With my brawny boyfriend, who holds a black belt in karate. He's due back at any moment. You'd better leave."

"Yeah, yeah, I'm goin'." The man meandered around the living room and took a quick peek into the kitchen. "Where's Willows buried? I wanna pay my last respects to the..." He scrunched his beady eyes and gave her a forced brown-toothed smile. "Gentleman."

"I have no idea. I'm new in town, and I'm not acquainted with the Willows's family history. You'll have to ask his grandson. He's downstairs in the bookstore." *I should have taken my pepper spray to the door with me.*

The man took his time sauntering out as if he was trying to test her patience. After he left, Heather slammed the door behind him and locked it. He wasn't the kind of person she'd imagined sitting in front of the fire with Chad's grandfather, drinking brandy and discussing rare books, unless they were forgeries. She hated to ponder the possibility, but for all she knew, maybe they were.

She ran to the kitchen, grabbed her cell phone, and tapped Chad's number.

He answered on the first ring. "Hi Heather."

The sound of his voice put her heart at ease. "There was a man up here inquiring about your grandfather. He's on his way to the bookstore."

"Thanks for letting me know. Talk to you later." Chad disconnected.

Heather ran to the living room window and pressed her forehead against it in an effort to see the front sidewalk. No good. She'd have to open it to get a better view. The room needed airing anyway. The scent of tobacco smoke hung around like a mackerel gone bad.

She pulled up the window sash and stuck her head out, but no one was on the sidewalk below. Maybe he was inside the bookstore. As she lifted her head, the panoramic, bird's-eye view of the west side of town became visible. In the distance, she spotted a familiar building.

The second-floor windows of the Willows family home were clearly visible, as was the entire side of the house with its glass patio doors that opened onto the sprawling yard. She recognized the distinctive architecture from when she and her aunt had attended a barbeque there last Sunday.

A sudden rapping on the front door startled her again. Heart pounding, she closed the window and turned to answer it. But this time she wasn't taking any chances. "Who's there?"

"Chad."

Unlocking the door, she opened it.

Chad sauntered in and gazed around. "I thought you said a man was coming to the bookstore to ask about my grandfather."

"That's where I sent him. He seemed a little skeptical when I told him Mr. Willows had passed away. He was strangely interested in where your grandfather was buried, but since I didn't know, I told him to ask you."

"What did this guy look like?"

"Around sixty-five, maybe seventy, with gray hair and a wrinkled face, probably from years of smoking. The man reeked of tobacco."

Chad sniffed. "I can still smell it."

"He wore a brown leather bomber jacket, like the kind you see in WWII movies. I thought he might be a homeless man wanting a handout, but he didn't ask for one." Heather bit her bottom lip as she tried to recall more details. "And he said he'd been here before."

Chad scrunched his eyes. He evidently didn't have a clue to the man's identity. "He might be a friend of my grandfather's. He'd made a lot of them that I'd never met."

"The man didn't appear friendly. And he sounded annoyed your grandfather wasn't here. Are there any other unsavory family *friends* I should be aware of who might come knocking on my door?"

Chad did a slow, steady, shake of his head. "Not sure what my grandfather was up to in the last five years. Like I told you, I only moved back to town a few weeks ago to help my sister with the bookstore."

"What do I do if anyone else comes looking for him?"

"If you don't recognize the person at the door, call me. I'll take care of it."

Heather had always been able to take care of things herself, but in this case, she was delighted to let the tall, muscular, ex-P.I. handle any unsavory situation.

Her cell rang. She pulled it from her jeans pocket. The hotel's number came to the screen.

"Excuse me. I should take this call."

"I'll go."

"Please stay. I want to ask you about something in the apartment. *I shouldn't have a problem coming up with a reason for him to hang around.*

"Hello?"

"Hi, it's Christine Talan at the Franklin House Hotel."

Heather held her breath. Hopefully, this call didn't have anything to do with her aunt's over-the-limit credit card. They'd already been though that hassle. "Is there something wrong?"

"Not at all. I called to inform you that three large fiberboard boxes came by train this morning with your name on them. The baggage man dropped the boxes off here before anyone could tell him you'd moved. They're located in the lobby by the check-in desk. Please pick them up at your earliest convenience."

"Thanks, I'll come by this morning."

"You might want to bring help. Like I said, they're large."

Heather ended the call. *Who would be sending me anything here?*

Chapter 6

THE only person Heather could ask for help, other than her aunt, leaned against the door jamb, his arms folded across his chest.

"The call was from Christine at the hotel. She said some large boxes were delivered there for me and to bring help. Could you possibly...?"

She didn't have to say the words. Chad's easy smile told her he was happy to assist. "There's a local writer's group meeting in the store for the next hour, so my sister won't be alone, in case my grandfather's *friend* should show up. But then, there's always Makki."

Heather opened the door. "He's a cute cat, but I can't imagine how he could help."

"He's feisty... and protective of my sister. You'd be surprised at the amount of damage he can do."

"I've had cats. I wouldn't be the least bit surprised."

Chad walked with her to where his Lexus was parked behind the building. "Let's take my car. There's more room than your rental."

She had to agree about the room, but how large could these boxes possibly be?

***

In the hotel lobby, Heather checked the return labels on the boxes. They were all from her ex, Jack Steele. She helped Chad load them into his car. *Jack probably hired someone to pack up my things and get them out of his condo to make room for another girlfriend to move in. He certainly didn't waste any time. Thoughtful of him to save me a trip. But then again, Jack was never this thoughtful, this forgiving, or this generous.*

Chad pulled his car up to her apartment entrance, and darted around the back. He dragged out a dolly to haul the boxes upstairs.

Heather climbed the stairs ahead of him to unlock the door.

Chad rolled in the first box. "Where do you want me to put this?"

"Set it down in my bedroom. I'll unpack it later." She tried not to sound as excited as she felt, being in desperate need of a change of clothes. She'd been washing and wearing the same ones for over a week, the only clothes she'd hastily flung into a suitcase in her frenzied state when she walked out on Jack.

It was a fortunate thing she'd been wearing her *Louboutin* sandals. At least she already had those.

Heather instructed Chad to put the other two boxes in the living room. After setting the last one down, he sauntered back to the front door and breathed deeply as he wiped the sweat from his brow. "If you need help getting rid of those huge boxes, let me know."

"Thanks, but I'll keep them. They'll come in handy when my aunt and I move out in a few months. Won't you stay for a... a cup of coffee or a drink of um, something... cool?"

"Not right now. I have to help Ashley in the book-store." His lips curved into a sensual smile as his eyes studied her face. "But I'll take you up on your offer another time."

Her heart flipped. "I look forward to it." *Why does he make me as jittery as a schoolgirl on her first date?*

Closing the door behind him, Heather shook off the feeling and went in search of a sharp blade. Sifting through the junk drawers, she found a thin piece of plastic with raised buttons. "Looks like it could be a remote."

She put it next to the flat screen TV in the living room, then continued to rummage through the rest until she found a cutter.

Heather slit the taped ends of the box in the living room and pulled out a large plastic bag with some of her clothes balled up inside.

"My best outfits!"

She carefully cut the top of the bag open.

The scents of bitter orange, cedar, sandalwood, and patchouli overwhelmed her sinuses. "Amouage!"

"The rat! He must have poured it over everything. I knew he'd try to get back at me for walking out on him, but this is too much!"

Grabbing her cell, she searched for a solution. *The Willows Bend Dry Cleaners* was two blocks away. She twisted the top of the plastic bag into a knot, and lugged it to the front door where she flung it down the stairs.

Ten minutes later, she opened the door to the cleaners. A balding, gray haired man behind the counter eyed her and her bag with interest. The name tag on his vest read Harry.

"What can I do for you?"

"Can you get the fragrance out of these clothes?"

He opened the bag, took a whiff, and raised his bushy gray eyebrows before closing the bag again.

"Whew! What happened? Did a bottle of after-shave break?"

"You guessed it. Can you get the smell out?"

"Depends on how saturated the clothes are." Harry's light blue eyes scanned the bag. "I'll do my best, but it'll cost ya."

Probably more money than I have to spare right now. She dug through the bag. "What if I leave you only a few things, to see if you can get the scent out?"

"Fair enough." He grabbed the clothes she selected, put them in another plastic bag, and then took her name and phone number.

Maybe I can get the scent out of the rest of the clothes myself. She resigned herself to spending the day doing laundry.

***

At 4:35, the front door opened.

Heather, who'd been washing her intimates in the bathroom sink, peeked into the living room to see her aunt on the sofa.

"Why didn't you call me to pick you up?"

"I got a lift from a friend." Julia flung off her walking shoes.

"What friend?"

Without answering, Julia sniffed the air and pinched her nostrils. "Whew! Did Chad take a bath in his after-shave?"

Even with the windows open, there was no getting rid of Jack's scent.

"It's not Chad's." Heather explained what had happened that morning.

Julia stuck her head out the window and sucked in a breath. "Isn't that just like Jack? I hope you gave him a piece of your mind."

"No. I refuse to give him the satisfaction of knowing he's infuriated me, even if I have to dump all my clothes in the trash to do it."

"Kind of radical, isn't it?"

Heather folded her arms in determination. "It is. But I can't let him know he's gotten to me."

"Have you tried washing your clothes to get the smell out?"

"I've done several loads of wash with scented laundry detergent, added vinegar to the rinse cycle, and even sprayed them with diluted Vodka before hanging them in front of the open windows to air. Nothing's worked yet. But I haven't heard from the dry cleaners. He may have gotten the smell out of the clothes I left with him."

Julia waved a hand in front of her face. "We can't stay here unless this apartment is fumigated. How have you lasted this long?"

"Guess I've gotten used to the smell."

Julia walked toward the hall. "I've got an idea." She opened the back door and stuck her head out. "There's a staircase that leads to an attic. We can take your clothes up there to air. At least they'll be out of the apartment."

"But the attic isn't ours to use. And the door's probably locked."

"Honestly, Heather, for a young woman, you can be such a ninny at times. Maybe it's open." Julia climbed up the stairs and turned the doorknob.

It wasn't.

Heather called Chad on her cell. "Hi, would it be possible for me to lease your attic?"

"What for?"

"I need to air out some things."

He hesitated a moment. "My grandfather's belongings are up there. It'll be crowded. How much room do you need?"

"Not much. And I only want to use it for a short time."

"I guess it'll be okay. I'll be right up with the key."

She couldn't let him find out she'd made his grandfather's apartment nearly uninhabitable after living in it for one day. "No, I'll come down."

"I'm already on my way."

A short time later, she met him at the top of the stairs. He handed her the key.

"I appreciate this. You can add the cost to next month's rent."

"Don't mention it. You can use the attic as long as you need to. Is there anything I can help you with?"

"No. Thanks. My aunt's here. We can handle it." Heather didn't want to be rude, but she couldn't let him in. "Thanks again." She opened the door a sliver, and squeezed inside, closing it behind her.

Climbing the back stairs, she handed her aunt the key. Julia unlocked the door and scurried to the window on the far side of the long room to open it. "There's another window on the opposite side. We have ventilation."

Heather opened the other one. "This might work." A hefty breeze blew in, and a swirl of dust caught in her throat. She coughed. "Except for the dust."

"What's a little dust? You'll have to wash your clothes again before you can wear them anyway."

Heather couldn't argue with that. They spent the next half-hour dragging clothes up the stairs and hanging them over the make-shift clothes lines Julia had strung between the low rafters. After the last blouse was hung, they locked the door and descended back to the apartment.

Heather sniffed the living room. "It smells better in here already."

Julia pinched her nose. "Are you kidding?"

She was right. "We'll have to eat out."

"I already have an engagement for dinner."

"With who?"

Julia smirked. "I'm not a child, and you're not my mother. I don't have to tell you everything. If we're gonna live in the same apartment, you'll to have to afford me some privacy. And I'll do the same for you."

Heather agreed. It was probably for the best. Although she'd vowed to keep an eye on her aunt, the woman did need privacy.

Why did that worry her?

Chapter 7

JULIA spent the next ten minutes on the phone and then she changed her clothes and came out wearing the same colorful, red, orange, and yellow outfit she'd worn when Heather had first seen her here. While her aunt was far from a devoted follower of fashion, Heather had to admit she still had a pretty good figure for a woman in her early fifties, and her own unique style of dress. Albeit a bit loud at times.

Julia grabbed her purse and swung the front door open. "Goodbye, dear. See you later."

Heather waved to her aunt as the woman scurried out. *With all Aunt Julia has been through today, I can't understand why she'd want to go out to dinner.*

Is it any of my business?

Yes.

I told my mom I'd keep an eye on her while we were here. If something happens, I'll never forgive myself—neither will the rest of the family. Of course, I'll get blamed, just like always, because I should have shown better judgment.

Julia had gotten involved with some pretty shady men in the past. "I hope this isn't another one."

Heather peeked out the front window to check the street below. Julia stood alone on the front sidewalk near the curb. A few moments later, a silver-gray SUV pulled up, and Julia got in. It made a left turn and headed north on 7th Avenue.

"I wonder what restaurants are down that way."

Heather opened her laptop and checked the dining places in Willows Bend. The Vendeglo Hungarian-style Restaurant came up with an address on that street. *Is that where she's headed? Does this have something to do with the Hungarian man she told me about?*

"I have to find an excuse to be there. But if I go alone, she'll think I'm following her."

Heather checked the closing time on the bookstore for Wednesday. It closed at six o'clock. "Great. It's a little after six now." She tapped Chad's name from her contact list.

It rang twice.

"Hi, Heather."

"Hi, I was wondering if you'd like to take me up on that rain check?"

"Sure."

"Are you still in the bookstore?"

"Yes, but I was about to drive my sister home."

"I want to take you both out to dinner."

"Are you sure you want us *both?*"

Was that confusion or disappointment in his voice?

He cleared his throat. "I mean, what did you have in mind?"

I hope they like Hungarian food.

***

The home-style restaurant reeked with the pungent aromas of Old World Europe, or what Heather imaged it would have smelled like if she'd ever been there.

"Why did you want to come here?" Chad asked.

Heather couldn't say it was to keep an eye on her aunt. "I suddenly had a taste for Goulash. This is the only restaurant in town that serves it. I checked their menu online."

"You made a superb choice," Chad said. "Their food is excellent. Our grandparents were friends of the owners. We'd eat here a couple times a month when we were kids, but we haven't been here is ages. The last I heard, their two grandsons were running the place now."

Ashley sighed. "Yeah, Miklos is *hot!*" She put a hand to her forehead and wiped imaginary sweat away. "Sandos, his older brother, *not so much.*"

Chad waved to someone at the back of the restaurant. Heather couldn't see who it was, but she hoped it wasn't her aunt.

A twenty-something man with strong shoulders, a sexy swagger, and a slightly superior smile approached them. He stopped and shook Chad's outstretched hand. "Haven't seen you in a while. Ever since the um... you know. Heard you'd moved to Chicago."

No doubt he was referring to Chad's breakup with his then fiancée, underwear model Krystal Stamos.

"Yeah, I thought it was for the best to leave. But I'm back now, helping my sister with the bookstore."

Miklos gazed down into Ashley's eyes. "Hi, Gorgeous."

It was the kind of flattery women fell for every time.

"Sorry about your granddad," he said. "And of course, the death of his friend, Esther, this morning."

"Thanks," Ashley said in a low voice, attempting to sound cool as her lips trembled. "Oh, by the way, this is our friend Heather Stanton."

Miklos's intense, coffee-colored gaze met Heather's as his lips curved into a jaunty smile. "Hello, I'm Miklos Vendeglo. Welcome to my family's restaurant."

Heather couldn't help but smile back. She could understand why Ashley thought he was *hot*. He was—in a roguish kind of way—with his dark, smoldering eyes. Like there might've been a pirate somewhere among his family's ancestors.

Miklos's gaze moved to Chad. "Are you going to Krystal's dad's funeral tomorrow?"

Chad's eyes widened. *He probably wasn't expecting that question.* "Not a good idea."

"Maybe you should. Krystal might need a strong shoulder to lean on."

"I'm sure yours will do nicely." Chad grinned.

Miklos raised an eyebrow. "But aren't you two back together? I mean, isn't that why she's staying in town?"

"We're not. Word on the street is Krystal's taking over her dad's off-track betting business. She's having a grand re-opening party on Saturday for the Kentucky Derby."

"Yeah, I heard about the grand re-opening. Sounds like fun."

Heather put a hand on her stomach. *I wish these two would stop talking about Chad's ex. I'm losing my appetite.*

Miklos pointed from Heather to Chad. "Are you two dating?"

Chad didn't answer.

Heather said, "No."

Chad's jaw tightened as his head motioned toward the inside of the restaurant. "Can we get a table?"

"Sure." Miklos grabbed the handles of Ashley's chair and wheeled her in front of them as he led the way through the electronic glass doors to a round table with a wide, red umbrella on the back patio.

"With this lovely weather, I thought you might like to eat *al fresco*. It's stuffy inside."

Pushing a restaurant chair aside, he tucked Ashley's front wheels under the tabletop. "I hope you're comfortable here. If not, I can move you."

Ashley's warm smile beamed up at him. "No, I'm fine."

"Great. Then I'll bring your drinks. Fröccs all around?"

Ashley and Chad nodded their approval.

"What's that?" Heather asked.

"Wine mixed with soda water. And since Hungarian wines are so delicious, so is fröccs. It's the perfect drink to have on a warm evening like this."

"Sounds tasty." She'd try any type of drink once.

Miklos disappeared inside the restaurant. Chad nudged his sister's chair. "You can stop drooling now."

"I'll drool if I want to." She grinned at her brother.

Listening to brother and sister talk about Ashley's love life was not helping her find her aunt. Giving the restaurant a quick scan through the glass patio doors proved fruitless. There were only a few people at the tables, but none were dressed like her aunt, and her flaming-red hair was hard to miss.

Chad turned his head in Heather's direction. "Are you looking for someone?"

"No, just getting a feel for the place. It has a lot of atmosphere."

Ashley adjusted her chair. Evidently, Miklos had shoved it a little too far under the table. "Granddad told me he used to bring Esther here for dinner. Rest their souls. Afterward they'd visit Madam Z for advice."

Advice? Heather had to ask, "What kind of advice does she dispense?"

Chad leaned back in his chair and crossed his arms. "A lot of nonsense."

Ashley ignored her brother's comment. "The Madam dabbles in the occult." She wrinkled her nose at him. "You don't believe in anything she says or does."

"Darn right I don't."

"Grandfather did, and there are a lot of other people in this town who do." Ashley motioned to the back of Madam Z's studio. "Three of them are coming out now."

Two gray-haired men, whose wrinkled skin and slow, unsteady gates made them appear to be pushing eighty, and one, thin, silver-haired woman, possibly a little younger, made their way to the senior citizens van parked in the lot.

Heather didn't believe in the occult either. But it might be the reason her aunt came here, looking for a way to rid herself of the curse.

Chapter 8

A few moments later, Miklos came back with the drinks. Heather resolved not to involve herself in her aunt's problems tonight and to focus on having a pleasant dinner with new friends.

Chad was right about the food—the Goulash tasted amazing.

After dinner, Miklos brought dessert and coffee to the table. Ashley had convinced her to order a *Dobos Torta*. How could she refuse? The photo of it on the menu looked so yummy.

Chad's was gone in less then five minutes. Ashley took time enjoying hers as she soaked up the attention Miklos paid her. Heather eyed her slice of caramel-frosted, multi-layered cake. How could she ever afford to eat all those calories? She sliced off a piece with her fork and took an experimental mouthful. *Mmmm. I'm hooked. Guess I'll hit the gym tomorrow.* Good thing she still had two days left on her trial membership.

As Heather enjoyed her latte, a smartly-dressed waiter brought the check. Miklos tore it up. "This evening's on me. Thanks for reacquainting me with your lovely sister, Chad."

The gleam in Ashley's eyes told Heather she was smitten.

Everyone thanked him. Heather was especially thankful. She'd invited Chad and his sister to dinner and would have had to pay for it, which wouldn't ordinarily be a problem, but with her recent clothing expenses, her funds were limited at the moment.

On their way out, Chad stopped in front of a man only a few inches taller than Heather's five-foot six. The robust young man patted Ashley's cheek. "Always a pleasure to see you again."

Chad put his hand out. "Heather, I'd like you to meet Sandos Vendeglo."

Sandos held Heather's gaze, and it was almost as if his brother was looking back at her. While his features were not as handsome, the family resemblance was unmistakable, especially those deep-set, dark eyes. But while Miklos was several inches taller than his older brother, and at least ten pounds thinner, Sandos was built solid, like a weight-lifter.

He took Heather's petite hand in his bear paw. "Nice to meet you."

Heather shook it and smiled as she eyed the long, thin snake tattoo on his right forearm. "Nice to meet you too, Mr. Vendeglo."

"Call me Sandy. Everyone does." His eyes gave her the once-over. Then he nudged Chad in the ribs. "You lucky dog."

Heather waited for Chad say they were only friends, but without a word, Chad grinned at him and continued to usher them down the aisle toward the front door.

Before she left, Heather spotted her aunt seated at a small table near the bar with a gray-haired man wearing a brown bomber jacket. The same man who'd come by the apartment to ask about Chad's grandfather. It figured she'd hook up with him. Or maybe he hooked up with her. In either case, it wasn't a favorable omen. Not that Heather believed in such things.

She rushed outside while they were in deep in conversation. Pointing the man out to her companions was probably not a good idea. If her aunt caught her spying, she'd never trust her again, and Chad would probably make a point of going back inside to talk to the man.

***

Sitting in the front seat of Chad's Lexus, Heather stared at his profile against the rays of the setting sun. *Such an attractive man. Still can't figure out why he doesn't want to date me. Sandy thought I was hot.*

As they rounded the corner near the bookstore, Ashley tapped Heather's shoulder from the back seat. "Thanks for inviting us to dinner. I haven't been out in a long time. It was fun. And it was great seeing Miklos again."

Heather couldn't help smiling at Ashley's beaming face. "You're welcome."

Chad pulled the car up to her door near the street. "I enjoyed the evening too. Maybe we can do it again... um, sometime. I mean, the three of us."

That was awkward. "I'm looking forward to it."

She wouldn't mind ending this evening with a kiss. But this wasn't a date. It was a chance to find out where her aunt had gone to dinner. So why did it feel like a date?

When he didn't offer to walk her to her door, she said, "Goodnight," got out of the car, and made her way upstairs.

Opening the door, she took an investigative sniff. With all the windows open, the smell was almost gone.

She went into the bedroom to put her purse away, but the scent still lingered in there.

"I need to buy air cleaner."

She grabbed her car keys and scampered down the stairs.

***

Back from the supermarket, Heather pulled into a parking space behind the bookstore just as her aunt got out of the silver-gray SUV. It was unfortunate she couldn't see who drove the car. And it was gone before she caught the license number.

Heather took the back stairs two at a time and made it to the apartment as her aunt walked in the front door. Giving her breath a quick catch, she sprayed the air in the kitchen and then headed for the living room with her spray bottle in hand.

"Aunt Julia!" She tried to sound surprised. "I didn't hear you come in."

Julia dropped her purse on the end table. "I just got home."

Heather pressed the trigger a few times to spray the area around her. "I bought air cleaner, hoping it would get rid of whatever scent is left."

Julia sniffed. "Smells like it's doing a good job. There's a slight scent, but I can live with it." She plopped on the sofa, kicked off her shoes, and checked her watch. "What's on TV tonight?"

"Don't know. I seldom watch TV."

Julia played with the remote device. "What's the matter with this? It doesn't turn on the TV. It doesn't turn on music. It doesn't turn anything on."

"Maybe it's broken or needs batteries. I'll ask Chad about it in the morning. Meanwhile, we can talk."

"About what?"

She wanted to ask about where her aunt went to dinner and who the man was, but there was the privacy issue. So, she asked, "Have you discovered anything new about Esther Kwinn's death?"

Julia picked at the red polish on her nails. "From what I overheard this morning, and then later at the police station, they're presuming she was killed with a blunt object to the side of her head, before being buried in the shallow grave. It was definitely *murder*. And from the way Detective Lindsey grilled me, you'd think I killed the woman, when all I did was poke her with my spade. But she was already dead by then."

At least her aunt had an alibi. "You were here with me all night and this morning, so Detective Lindsey should have eliminated you right away."

"You'd think so, wouldn't you?"

"When you arrived at the park, did you see anyone suspicious?"

Julia tilted her head in thought. "Like I told the police, the only thing I saw was the Willows Bend Senior Citizen's van parked by the field house. They're checking it out, but from what I hear, it's usually there Thursday mornings."

She stood. "It's a huge park. The killer or killers could have been hiding behind a tree, or under the stone bridge by the lagoon, and I wouldn't have seen them."

Julia pulled out her cell phone.

"Who are you calling?"

"Christine Talan. Esther was her neighbor for ten years. She might have some ideas why Heather was in the park early that morning." Julia grabbed her purse from the end table. "Then I'm going to take a warm, relaxing bubble bath, and give everything a hard think before I go to bed. Maybe my subconscious will remember something my conscious mind has blocked out." She sauntered to her room and closed the door.

Heather hated the fact her aunt was involved in another homicide, but right now there was nothing she could do. She'd have to wait and see how things played out. Hopefully, they wouldn't turn out as badly as they did the last time her aunt found a dead body.

Heather opened her laptop and checked her marketing website. Nothing yet. But this was only her second day in business. Usually, her marketing strategies worked almost as fast as the lightning that streaked across the night sky. Maybe she was too impatient. She'd wait another day. People were busy.

***

A creaking noise woke Heather out of a light sleep. Slipping out of bed, she groped her way to the hall, not daring to turn on the light for fear it might be seen by a prowler. She didn't like venturing out into the darkness, but something had to be done.

Heather let her cell phone light guide her as she inched her way to the kitchen, where she grabbed a skillet from the sink's drain board.

Outside, the previously heavy rain had settled to a gentle drizzle, and her apartment was full of a kind of deafening silence.

Another creaking noise came toward her from the hall. Her heart jumped to her throat. For a breathless moment, she stood there, unable to move, nerves keyed for more sounds. Around her again was that dreadful silence—a silence that chilled her to the bone. In a fraction of a second, the entire room was illuminated as though a floodlight had been turned on. It was only a flash of lightning, but the flash showed a dark figure lurking at the back door.

Giving the figure an intense stare, she could barely make out who it was. *Aunt Julia?* She let out the breath she'd been holding. *Sleepwalking again?*

Heather put the frying pan on the counter and followed Julia, at a distance, down the back stairs. Her aunt walked toward the end of the gravel-filled alley. Julia placed a tiny object on the ground. Then she stomped it with her shoe, chanting some words over and over. After the chanting stopped, she chugged something from a tiny vial, as if she was tossing back a shot of whiskey.

Heather's breath hung heavy in the humid night air as she pressed herself against the darkness under the stairs, waiting for Julia's next move.

Trailing behind, Heather followed Julia back into the apartment.

She spent the rest of the night trying to find a comfortable sleeping position while worrying about her aunt. *The sleepwalking's getting worse. I have to confront her about it.*

Chapter 9

In the morning, Heather waited for her aunt to come out of her room. As Julia headed for the kitchen, she followed. "You need help."

Julia ambled toward the living room. "You're right. I can't find my walking shoes."

"They're under the sofa. But they're not what I'm talking about. You were sleepwalking again last night."

"No, I wasn't."

"I followed you out the back door and down the stairs around three in the morning."

"Oh that." Julia waved a hand as if to brush the words away. "How could I be sleepwalking when I hardly got any sleep at all?"

"Then what were you doing?"

Julia grabbed her shoes and slipped them on. "I'd tell you, but you're not open-minded enough to understand."

Heather folded her arms. "Try me."

Julia wandered the room for a few minutes with her eyes scrunched as if she was thinking it over. Then she stopped in front of Heather.

"I'll tell you." She raised her index finger. "But no judgments." Then she walked to the kitchen and poured herself a cup of French Roast.

Heather inched closer to her aunt. "I won't judge you. I only want to understand what's going on."

Julia stirred sugar into her cup and took a sip. "Where do I start?"

"Why don't you start by telling me what you were doing outside in the middle of the night."

"I was performing a ritual. And I had to do it last night because it was the only night this month with a full moon."

Unbelievable. "What kind of ritual?"

"The kind to obliterate... you know."

"Not the curse, again?"

Julia waved her hands in the air as she raised her voice, "I knew you weren't going to be open-minded about this. Why do I tell you *anything?*"

Heather squeezed her eyes shut in an effort to control her exasperation, and in the calmest voice she could muster said, "Sorry. I want to hear everything. How did you find out about this ritual?"

Julia hesitated as she put her coffee mug down. "Madam Z advised me to do it. She's an occultist, and Christine said she's excellent at helping people. Chris drove me to Madam's studio after she got off work yesterday. And I have to admit, the Madam knows her stuff. She dug deep into her bag of supernatural secrets and provided me with some of the mystifying tools I need to take the curse away."

She can't possibly believe this. "Did whatever she gave you work?"

"The Madam explained it takes time and patience to rid yourself of a curse. It's not something you can do in one night. Or with one ritual. This was only the preliminary one that protects me from slander and gossip."

"How much did this preliminary 'ritual' cost you?"

"Whatever was in my wallet."

Heather could tell where this was going—a slow drain of her aunt's finances.

Julia picked up the television remote and shoved it into Heather's hand. "Here. While I'm gone, see if you can fix this thing so I can watch some programs tonight."

***

Heather dropped her aunt off at the park and came back to the apartment. She struggled with the back of the little remote device, but it wouldn't come off. Slipping it into her jeans pocket, she headed for the bookstore. *Maybe Chad can do something with it.*

A handwritten sign taped to the window stopped her from reaching for the door handle. *Closed until noon today.*

Odd, neither Chad nor Ashley had mentioned they'd changed the store hours today. "I'll talk to him later."

She walked around the building to where her car was parked. Across the street, the elderly man in the brown bomber jacket stood on the corner smoking a cigarette. As she met his gaze, he dropped the cigarette and crushed it out with his scuffed, brown leather shoe.

Who is that man, and why is he watching us?

She pulled out her cell phone to take a quick snapshot, but the man hurried around the corner as if he was being chased. Heather rushed after him. The man glanced over his shoulder, and then he ducked into an alley.

Breathless, Heather stood at the entrance to the narrow passageway and checked out the area. Too many back doors, smelly overflowing trash containers, and no visible exit. Not an inviting scenario. *As much as I'd like to find out who he is, it's not worth going in there.*

Heather drove to the Franklin House Hotel and entered the hotel lobby expecting to find Christine, but Vikki Garret manned the front desk. Vikki pushed a lock of dark, curly hair from her high forehead as her pale brown eyes moved from the computer screen to Heather's face. She greeted her with the smile hotel clerks put on when they need to appear pleasant because it's part of their job.

"Can I help you, Ms. Stanton?"

"Hi. Please call me Heather. Is Christine Talan here?"

"Not right now. She should be back around noon. But if it's important, you might catch her at Nikos Stamos's funeral this morning."

Could Chad be there too? Is that why he closed the bookstore? Men! My aunt's right—you can't trust them.

As much as she'd like to find out if he was there, Heather had no desire to be anywhere near Krystal Stamos, Chad's ex. She'd already met the glamorous, arrogant, former underwear model in less than desirable circumstances. Besides, in her jeans and tank top, she wasn't dressed for the occasion. Nor could she change, since all her clothes still reeked of Jack's aftershave.

"I don't want to bother Christine while she's at a funeral. Maybe you can answer some questions for me."

Vikki crossed her arms. "If I can."

"Are you acquainted with Madam Z?"

"She's the elderly woman who has a studio next door to the Hungarian restaurant. Why are you asking?"

"I had dinner at the Vendeglo yesterday, and I noticed her name on a sign in the window next door. But I can't find out anything about her online."

"She's kind of mysterious. Doesn't have a website. Word is she won't have anything to do with computers, or any kind of technology, except for the telephone. Strictly old, old school—like writing with quill pen on parchment."

"What does she do in her storefront studio?"

"Dabbles in the occult and stuff like that." Vikki unfolded her arms. "A lot of older people in this town are her clients. She's into things they don't want to talk about, and she concocts all these magic elixirs. It's supposed to help with their problems. It all seems kind of weird to me."

"Sounds that way."

"I do see her in the supermarket, occasionally. She frightens me a little. I mean, her hair is as white as snow, and her pupils... like pinpoints." Vikki shivered.

"Do you have the name of anyone in town who's been seeing her?"

"I've seen several folks from the retirement village walk into her studio, but I couldn't tell you their names. And I remember seeing Esther Kwinn come out her back door more than once when my friends and I ate dinner on the outdoor patio at the restaurant."

"Do you eat there often?"

Vikki inched closer and raised an eyebrow. "A couple of girlfriends and I have a standing reservation for a table on Friday nights. The food's great, and Miklos is one of the hottest, and most eligible, guys in town, next to Chad Willows. But to be around Chad, we hang out at his bookstore. I know I spend too much money there."

Heather slanted a disparaging glance at her. *You and your friends might consider Chad hot, but I wouldn't consider him eligible. Not if I have anything to do with it.*

"Thanks for your help." Heather turned to leave, and then she turned back again as another question crossed her mind. "Has an elderly man, a smoker, who wears a brown bomber jacket checked into this hotel?"

Vikki's lips scrunched. "I haven't checked in anyone with that description, but then I only work here part-time. You might want to ask Christine. Everyone in this town is six degrees of separation from everyone else. Like the old guy who owns the cleaners, Harry, is a friend of Madam Z's. Esther took her dry cleaning to Harry's, and she also visits Madam Z, who always takes her clothes to Harry's, etcetera. See what I mean?"

"In other words, everyone knows everyone else." *And that information might help me find the guy in the bomber jacket. If he hasn't checked in here, then he might be living with someone in town. Someone who's back door is in that formidable alleyway.*

Chapter 10

HEATHER proceeded back to her apartment, parked herself on a kitchen stool, and checked her website for clients.

No emails yet. *How long does it take for word to spread?*

Since there was nothing else to do, she scanned a few websites and answered emails from her mom, her sister, and several of her former co-workers whom she still considered friends. One in particular caught her attention with the word, *Congrats*, in the subject line.

Hi Heather,

I admire you for opening your own marketing business, but be warned, your former boss now considers you competition. He's gotten a ton of emails about you from our clients, and he's telling everyone you're an unstable person and a poor business risk because you lost the company millions in fees. Sorry to have to tell you, but from what I hear, you're considered a pariah in the industry right now.

Heather stopped reading. She couldn't think. She couldn't breathe. Her new business had skidded to a screeching halt before it even started. How could the man she once admired, respected, and even considered a friend, say such cruel, untrue things about her?

She hated the confrontation she'd had with him. How he'd twisted her words to make her sound ridiculous and kept interrupting so she could barely get a word in, until her temper burst out, and there was nothing left to do but quit.

Hot blood rushed to her face as red flashed across her eyes. She picked up her unwashed coffee cup and lifted it over her head.

Throwing this cup isn't going to accomplish anything. Stop acting like you have the emotional maturity of a two-year-old.

She put the cup down and took a calming breath. It didn't work. So she took another and another, until she could finally think straight again.

"That sleaze ball needed a scapegoat, and I was convenient. I *should've* stayed and fought the allegations. I *could've* mounted a notable defense, and if I had, I probably *would've* won."

Could've, would've, should've. The three auxiliary verbs that always came up as an afterthought. She smiled at what might have been. But her smugness was short-lived. Her former boss wielded an excess of money and power. He'd make her appear so ridiculous, no one in the industry would talk to her ever again.

For all I know, he's probably already done it.

Heather jumped off the kitchen stool and shook her hands out in frustration. Then she got a Pepsi from the refrigerator and chugged it down. Caffeine and sugar always steadied her nerves, cleared her mind, and helped her to focus.

"I'll compose a scathing email. The lying, conniving, manipulating... um..." *I need one more strong word to complete the sentence.*

Instead of coming up with another, her subconscious told her, *What's the point? It'll only give him more ammunition to shoot you down.* She stared at the computer screen and spread her arms out in momentary defeat.

"What do I do now?"

As if in answer to her question, her cell rang. She swiped it without checking the caller ID, grateful for the distraction.

"Hi Heather, it's Christine Talan. Vikki said you wanted to talk to me."

"Yes, I do."

But every question she'd had on her mind earlier had vanished. Switching focus from her job momentarily moved her thoughts elsewhere. It took a couple of minutes to pull them together.

"Why did you take my aunt to see Madam Z?"

"Because Julia wants to rid herself of a curse. There isn't anyone in town who's better at getting rid of *obstacles to happiness* than the Madam."

This was hard to believe, but she'd have to delve into the subject of Madam Z another time. Right now, there was another matter she wanted to talk about.

"My aunt may try to involve you in investigating Esther Kwinn's murder. Please don't let her do it. I don't want to see harm come to you."

A short silence and quiet breathing. "I don't want to talk about it over the phone. People may be listening. Why don't you and your aunt come to my house for dinner tonight. Around six. I hope you like spaghetti."

Heather didn't have to think twice. Spaghetti was one of her favorite meals, and she'd do anything to keep her aunt out of trouble, even if she had to sacrifice her waistline to do it.

"We'll be there."

She ended the call and slipped her phone into her pocket next to the broken remote device. "If Christine's back, Chad must be too." Heather headed downstairs.

The sign on the bookstore door was gone, so she opened it. A sharp tinkle sounded as she walked in, followed by a loud *meow*.

Makki stood on the front counter and stared at her with his large, cat-green eyes, inviting her to pet him. As she did, his back rose to meet her hand. "And how are you today, sweetheart?"

"I'm good. How are you?"

Heather spun around. Chad stood behind her with a Cheshire-cat grin on his handsome face.

Heat rose to her cheeks. "I was talking to the cat."

"And I was answering for him. Now, what can I do for you?"

"I... um." She fumbled with the television remote before showing it to him. "This doesn't work. The back won't come off to replace the battery."

He glanced at the object. "What is it?"

"We're hoping it's the remote control for the living room TV. I found it in a kitchen drawer."

Chad took the rectangular, black device and studied it. "There's no logo to say what brand it turns on. But then again, my grandfather was kind of eccentric. He liked to collect things that weren't of any use to anyone. He'd fill drawers with piles of junk."

"And this could be one of them?"

"I wouldn't be surprised." He tossed it on the counter. "I might have stashed the remote for the living room television into the junk box I packed up and put in the attic." Chad's lips curved into an enigmatic smile. "I'll be glad to search for it."

Heather's heart quickened—partly from his smile and partly because she couldn't let him. The odor of Jack's aftershave still lingered up there.

"It's kind of you to offer, but on second thought, I can't afford a cable bill right now."

"No problem. You can still watch TV. I hooked up the free stations to the antenna on the roof after you agreed to take the apartment, so it won't cost you anything but the electricity."

"It was thoughtful of you to do that for us, but don't bother to go to the attic. I'll do it later. Thanks, anyway."

Chad put the remote into a drawer under the cash register. "Is there anything else?"

"There's one other thing. This morning when I left the apartment, the man I told you about was standing across the street, watching me. I tried to take a photo of him with my cell, but when he saw what I was doing, he turned the corner, ran down the street, and ducked into an alley. I didn't want to risk going after him because it didn't look safe, and I couldn't see an exit. So I left."

"At least you've got common sense. Following someone is a dangerous thing to do. The next time you feel like sleuthing, call me."

"You couldn't possibly have been there in time. Your store was closed until noon."

He turned his gaze to the window as he rubbed the back of his neck. "Yeah. Well, Ashley had a double session at rehab this morning, and I had something important to do."

Like comforting your ex-fiancée at her father's funeral, which you said you weren't going to attend?

Ashley rolled her wheelchair in from the back room. "Where's Makki? I can't find him." She made an abrupt stop beside Heather. "Hi. I thought I heard your voice. Have you seen Makki?"

"He greeted me when I walked in, and then he disappeared."

Ashley gazed at the ceiling. "He likes to climb to the top shelves and walk around up there. I hate when he does that. It makes me nervous. I'd rather have him safely down here with me. Chad, please take a look."

"He's perfectly safe up there. You shouldn't worry about him."

A moment later, Makkie jumped into Ashey's lap. "Where were you?" She hugged the squirming cat.

Heather's cell beeped a reminder. *Pick up dry cleaning.* She put it in her back pocket.

"I have an errand to run. Talk to you later."

She rushed out the door and hurried the two blocks to the dry cleaners. *I hope they were able to get Jack's aftershave out of my clothes.*

Chapter 11

THE elderly clerk retrieved Heather's dresses. "We were able to eliminate the fragrance." He hung them up on a hook near the counter.

Heather eyed her pale blue, silk Tribeca dress and lifted the plastic.

Then she gave the other clothes the sniff test. They all had a mild scent of cleaning solution, but at least the aftershave was gone. She paid the clerk and took the clothes back to her apartment. Taking the back stairs to the attic, she unlocked the door and opened it. Her breath caught.

"I can still smell it, but at least the scent's getting weaker."

She left the windows open, gathered up the clothes, and took everything downstairs in a huge bundle. This time she'd soak them in baking soda and vinegar for a couple of hours before washing in scented detergent again.

***

Later in the evening, Heather drove her aunt to the Talan's house, a modest architectural version of the Willows's enormous, gray brick home next door. Having been built on the back of the lot, the Talan house had a long front yard of neatly trimmed grass and a large garden with an abundance of spring flowers.

Heather parked a short distance from the front door. Julia got out of the car and inspected the red and white striped tulips planted below the large, bay window. "Aren't these lovely?"

"Yes, they are." Heather knocked.

Christine opened the door with a flourish.

"Hello and welcome. You're right on time. The table's set, and dinner's nearly ready."

As they entered the foyer, Heather handed Christine the bottle of Chianti she'd picked up at the liquor store on the way.

Christine led them into the dining room and set the bottle on the table. "This will go great with dinner."

Heather couldn't take her eyes from the multi-tiered, crystal chandelier glistening over the table. "What an elegant lighting fixture."

"A twenty-fifth wedding anniversary gift from the Willows family. They're so thoughtful and generous."

I've seen their palatial house. And so many businesses in this town with the Willows name on them, makes me wonder how wealthy they are.

A buzzer chimed. Christine quirked her head. "Pasta's ready."

Christine brought out everything she'd prepared for dinner.

"Help yourselves. We're not formal here. And there's plenty. I usually make enough spaghetti for an army so I don't have to cook every day."

Heather scooped up a clump of Spaghetti Bolognese and set it on her plate. Her aunt did the same. Then

Julia grabbed a slice of garlic bread from the plate in the middle of the table.

The smell was heavenly as butter oozed from each savory piece. Heather lifted two and set them on her plate. Julia scanned the room. "Is your husband joining us?" Christine took a seat next to Heather. "No. He's driving his truck to Michigan today." She served herself a plate of spaghetti as well. "I couldn't talk about my suspicions in front of George. He gets peeved at me if he even suspects I've stuck my nose into someone else's business. And I usually don't, but in the case of Esther Kwinn, I feel certain things need to be looked into."

Heather wound a forkful of spaghetti. "And you told them to the police?"

"You bet I did." Christine sniffed. "Esther told me the other day, in confidence, she thought a being was watching her."

"Did she tell you why, or who it might be?"

"No, but even when she was outside, she suspected an evil entity was listening in on her conversations.

Evil entity? "It sounds to me like she was being a little paranoid. Imagination can do strange things."

Julia waved her fork. "Or maybe she confronted the entity in the park, and it killed her."

I don't believe these two.

Christine lifted the garlic bread to her lips. "It must have been familiar with her habits."

Glancing at her aunt, Heather said, "You mean, someone like Madam Z?"

Julia poked a finger at her niece. "Don't say anything negative about her. She's the only person who can help me shake off my curse."

Heather closed her eyes, clenched her teeth, and let out a slow breath. *That curse again.*

Christine smiled. "She's exceptional at what she does, and she seems to have some kind of special powers."

Julia nodded in agreement. "She knew a lot about me even before I told her who I was."

"You were all over the local news last week. Everyone in town knows everything about you." Heather couldn't help saying the words with a sarcastic tinge to her voice.

Julia dabbed at her lips with a napkin. "I suppose you're right."

"Honestly, Aunt Julia, how can you believe another human being could rid you of something that doesn't exist in the first place?"

Christine clicked her tongue. "Are you implying Madam Z doesn't know what she's doing?"

It had occurred to me. Heather opened her mouth to speak, but Julia cut in, "I knew it. You're always jumping to the wrong conclusions about people."

I'm not the one who jumps to the wrong conclusions. Heather gulped down the rest of her wine along with the words before she started an argument with her aunt.

Julia scrunched her eyes as she glared at Heather. "What about the evil entity following Esther? If the police wouldn't help, her only alternative would be Madam Z."

"I can't see Detective Lindsey investigating evil spirits. Especially if it was a part of Esther's imagination."

Christine's lips puckered. "Then we'll have to do it ourselves. Won't we, Julia?"

"You got that right." Julia chomped down on a thick slice of garlic bread.

I have to talk sense into these ladies. But how can I, when they're so determined?

Chapter 12

H EATHER swallowed her last mouthful of spaghetti, put her fork down, and pushed her plate away. "You've convinced me. I'll help you." *I don't have anything better to do since my online marketing business tanked, and I haven't any other prospects at the moment.* At least this way she'd be able to keep on eye on what they were doing before they made nuisances of themselves.

Julia narrowed her eyes, giving Heather a tight stare. "But I thought you didn't want to have anything to do with it."

"I changed my mind."

"Great." Julia rubbed her hands together as if she were eager to start. "What do we do first?"

Christine's pale green eyes flashed with excitement. "We need to figure out what evil entity Esther was afraid of?"

"Speaking of *who* she might have been afraid of," Heather said, "are you familiar with a short, gray-haired man in his late sixties or early seventies who smokes cigarettes and wears a brown bomber jacket?"

But it was Julia who answered. "Sounds like the man I met in the Vendeglo restaurant the other evening.

Madam Z told me I'd make a new friend, and his name would begin with the letter B."

Julia flung her arms up in a gesture of astonishment. "And I did. His name was Bax. She said my instincts will tell me to be cautious, but my instincts will prove wrong. I should trust him, and I'll be rewarded."

Christine stood. "That's a description of Esther's first husband. Baxter Haven."

Finally, some information about this guy.

"Aunt Julia, how did you meet the man?"

"The madam said I would meet him accidently. And that evening, as I was moving my chair to leave the table at the Vendeglo restaurant, he tripped over my chair leg and practically fell into my lap. He apologized, of course, and then we talked for a while before he left."

That's why I saw them together. "Talked about what?"

"This and that." Julia patted her auburn tresses and blinked several times." He liked my hair and said I had kind eyes." She giggled. "And even though he was a great deal older than me, I gave him my number."

"Did you get his?"

Julia scrunched her face. "No."

Heather tapped a finger on the table—patience wasn't her strong point. "I don't like this whole situation. Madam Z tells you you're going to meet a man who's name begins with B. And then she tells you he's going to be your new friend and you should trust him? Really, Aunt Julia?"

"Are you saying, he was deliberately sent to meet me?" Julia tsked. "You're such a skeptic."

"I'm surprised you're not. I never knew anyone who could predict the future with that much accuracy."

"I told you she was good."

"No one's that good."

Julia jutted her chin out as if she'd been insulted. "*She is.*"

Christine picked up Heather's empty plate. "I'll clear the table and serve dessert."

Over blueberry pie and coffee, Heather explained to Christine why she was interested in Bax.

"It sounds like he was an associate of Chad's grandfather." Christine said. "I hate to admit it, because I liked the man, but some of his friends were kind of seedy-looking. Like people who lived on the streets."

Julia stirred sugar into her coffee. "A lot of Bax's words were Chicago street slang." She let out a long, slow sigh. "Gees, they made me homesick."

Heather couldn't help missing the delights of Chicago herself—the gourmet restaurants, the concerts at Symphony Center and Grant Park, the wind in her hair as she sailed on the *Long Ship Wendy* across Lake Michigan.

As a once successful marketing executive, she was used to living the good life. Now she needed to manage on a much tighter budget, so she was better off in Willows Bend. It took money to live in luxury, and she wasn't exactly rolling in it at the moment.

Shaking off her feelings, she focused on Esther's death. "Christine, would you know of anyone who had a motive to kill Esther?"

Christine moved her head from side to side. "I have no idea. But there's one person in this town who might."

Heather closed her eyes. "Don't tell me it's Madam Z?"

Christine's doorbell rang.

Chapter 13

HEATHER rose to her feet. "Are you expecting company? Should we leave?"

Christine chuckled. "Don't be silly. It's only Chad. I invited him over for coffee after he dropped off Ashley at the rehab center. After her session, she's getting her lovely black hair washed and blown out next door at the salon for her date with Miklos Vendeglo."

So he was sincere about liking Ashley, even though his words were the most shallow I've ever heard from any guy. Guess this is one point in his favor.

"But I thought her boyfriend was that computer geek, Kyle Edwards." Julia said.

"No. I believe they're just friends. But who knows? In my opinion, Kyle is a much better match for her. He's not as handsome, of course, but then few young men are."

"Few young men are what?" Chad walked in wearing the smile that always gave Heather a warm glow. "Hi, Everyone."

Christine pulled a chair out across from Heather. "I was saying how few young men are as handsome as Miklos Vendeglo."

"Oh, him." Chad didn't sound enthusiastic.

"Sit," Christine said. "I'll be right back with your coffee. Help yourself to pie."

Chad planted himself in the chair. He grabbed a napkin from the table and patted his face. "It's a little humid outside. I hear we're in for more rain."

"What luck." Julia said. "That means I'll be doing community service at the retirement village instead of the park. I can snoop around without anyone suspecting me."

He scrunched the napkin into a ball. "Snoop around?"

Christine set Chad's coffee cup on the table. "Julia and I are investigating Esther's murder on our own."

Chad glanced at the two conspirators. "I wouldn't advise it."

Heather lifted her coffee cup in her aunt's direction. "Tell him your reason."

"Christine told the police Esther suspected she was being followed by an evil entity, and they did nothing about it."

"What?" He sounded as if he didn't hear correctly.

"That's what we'd like to know," Christine and Julia said simultaneously. Then they both said, "Jinx!"

Heather nearly choked on her coffee. "Come again?"

"If two people say the same thing at the same time, they're jinxed." Julia's hand struck her cheek. "Now I'm not only cursed, I'm jinxed!"

Chad covered his mouth, obviously to hide a grin. And who could blame him? The high pitch of Julia's voice made her sound like a silly school girl.

"I believe the correct term for jinx is synchronicity," he said. "Existing or occurring at the same time. So, what's this about a curse?"

He would pick up on that. This conversation is getting ridiculous. "My aunt thinks she's been cursed with a shroud of death, along with misfortune for the rest of her days."

Julia shook a finger at Heather. "I don't think it. I'm positive all the recent deaths in town have occurred because of the curse." She jumped to her feet. "I have to talk to Madam Z about the jinx. She's the only one who can help me."

Julia grabbed her purse and pulled out rose-colored lip gloss. "Thanks for dinner, Christine. Would the Madam be in her studio now?"

Christine checked the wall clock. "It's only seven-thirty. She's usually there until eight on most weeknights. If not, ring the bell. She lives upstairs."

Julia glazed her lips with gloss as she made her way to the front door. "Heather, will you drive me?"

Chad got to his feet and studied Heather's face. "You're not condoning any of this, are you?"

"Any of what?"

His brow furrowed. "For one, Christine and your aunt investigating Esther's murder. They could make trouble for the police... or worse. Didn't you learn anything from the last time you and your aunt investigated a death on your own?"

Yes, but that was different. She'd make sure things didn't deteriorate this time. He couldn't possibly think she approved of what they were doing.

Heather grabbed her purse. "Can we talk later? My aunt wants to go to Madam Z's before she closes."

"And that's another thing." Disapproval tugged at the corners of his lips. "You don't believe in any of her mumbo-jumbo, do you?"

Julia opened the front door. "Come on, Heather. It's getting late."

Before Heather could answer his question, she'd have to see what the mumbo-jumbo was about for herself. "Sorry, gotta go."

***

The lights in the window of the storefront next door to the Vendeglo restaurant shone dimly, indicating Madam Z might still be open to visitors. Julia got out of the car and walked toward the restaurant.

Heather pointed. "Her studio's the other way."

Julia tapped her niece's shoulder. "Would you please find out if she has time to see me tonight?"

"Why don't you go in yourself?"

"I didn't make an appointment." Julia's newly glazed lips drew into a sad smile. "Please do me this one favor?"

"I'll do it, but only because I want to see what kind of influence she has over you for myself. Where will you be?"

"In the restaurant getting fortified with a quick shot of something from the bar."

What could possibly be so scary about this woman that would make my aunt, the bravest woman I know, be intimidated by her?

Heather approached the iron-studded oak door of the building next door to the restaurant, sucked in a breath to ready herself for anything she might encounter, and turned the handle. The door opened with a creak, a squeak, and a long groan.

As she stepped into the quaint boutique-style shop, tendrils of incense curled around the room. The walls and surfaces were crowded with colorful candles, books on shelves, miniature shrines, tapestries, and crystals of every shape, size, and color.

She waved the incense smell away with her hand and made her way to a bookshelf to read the titles:

From Alchemy to Wicca.

The Black Arts.

Mystical Practices Throughout the Ages.

Under a clear glass counter was a thin volume with gilded pages. The book lay open to a graphic picture of people writhing in pain on one side and a snake slithering across some occult symbols on the other. *Where have I seen that snake before?*

"What are you doing there?" A voice shrieked.

Heather shuddered. The high-pitched, choppy words stabbed her ear drums. Heart racing, she put a hand to her chest as a slim, elderly woman dressed in a black, satin robe approached her. The woman couldn't have been more than five feet tall, with tight lips and a haggard, pale face. Her thinning white hair, worn in a tight bun on top of her head, added a ghoulish touch to her appearance.

She rushed over and closed the tome with a thud, revealing the title in calligraphic gold lettering. *The Pleasure Garden of Shadows.*

A pair of highly menacing hazel eyes pierced Heather with laser focus. "I thought the door was locked. But now you're here, what do you want?"

"I'm looking for Madam Z."

The woman's snow-white eyebrows twitched. She rubbed her gnarled hands together in a business-like manner.

"I am she. What is your problem?"

"I'm not here for myself."

"Are you sure?" The madam circled Heather, silver pentagram earrings dangling near her chin. Her gaze fixated on the top of Heather's head and slowly moved to her feet. "I see an extremely troubled aura around you. Something about a man."

Heather flattened her lips. *Chad.*

"No, two men. Am I right?"

Heather's hands squeezed into fists. *And my former boss.*

Madam rubbed her sharp chin. "Possibly three, yes?" *Jack.*

Heather scrunched her eyes trying to scrutinize the woman. *She's only guessing.* "No. I'm here to inquire for my Aunt Julia. She'd like to consult with you this evening if you have time."

"I had a feeling she would come, so I cleared my schedule to focus only on her special problem."

I'm sure you did. "If you ask me, the whole thing is absurd. I don't believe in curses."

Madam Z snickered. "They're real to the people who do. I *help* get rid of them. Or what people believe them to be."

"By having them perform idiotic rituals which can't possibly do anything but make them appear ridiculous?"

"What I tell my clients to do is extremely powerful."

Heather had to stop herself from rolling her eyes. Indignant emotions bubbled to the surface. Did Madam Z think she was stupid? She hated seeing victims duped by such ludicrous tripe, and then being charged a phenomenal fee, draining them of their money, because they were too afraid to do anything without consulting her.

It almost ruined her friend's life. Luckily, she was able to talk sense into the girl before she lost her inheritance to a charlatan. She won't allow it to happen to her aunt.

"That's a lot of nonsense! And trying to convince people it's true is not only absurd—it can be dangerous."

Madam Z tilted her white head as if she didn't understand Heather's reasoning. "On the contrary." She kept her voice low and even. "There's nothing ludicrous about making people feel better. Nor is it harmful. The important thing is a person's peace of mind."

"For a price!" Heather stomped to the door. It wouldn't open, so she turned around. "Your door's locked. I'd like to leave."

"When we solve your problem, you can go."

"You can't keep me here. And I told you, I don't have a problem." The words came out louder and more determined than she meant them to.

Madam Z ambled to the counter and opened a ruby-colored, square box covered in gold Chinese symbols and lifted out a tiny white feather. She strolled over to Heather and pressed the plume into her hand. "Some advice."

"How much will it cost?"

"I don't charge. I ask for donations."

"How much of a donation are you asking?"

"Whatever you have in your purse."

Where have I heard that before? How far is she going to take this? Heather stared at the feather as Madam Z spoke.

"You're troubled right now, and you're walking a fine line. On one side is happiness and abundance." She turned the white feather over to reveal the black side. "The other, mistrust and malice. Don't let your temper cause you to choose poorly."

The Madam closed Heather's fingers around the feather and placed her own hand over Heather's fist. "When your temper rises, take a cold bath with red rose petals in the water. It will cool your raging emotions."

Heather's flesh prickled. "That's a load of bull! We both know it."

She opened her hand, and the feather floated out.

"I'm not giving you one red cent for your unsolicited advice." With her pulse pounding, Heather charged out the, now open, door and ran into the restaurant, planting herself on a tall bar stool.

Julia downed what was left in her glass. "Will she see me?"

Heather slammed her fist on the black marble bar, but the hand that had held the feather wouldn't open. It took every ounce of self-control she had to keep her voice steady. "Yeah."

Julia jumped off the stool. "Great. Wait here. Have a drink. You look like you could use one."

The bartender approached her. "What'll it be?"

"Something cold." The words jumped out, to her surprise.

"Long Island Iced Tea?" The bartender suggested.

"Sounds good."

The audacity of that woman, acting like she knows anything about me. She had to be guessing at my problems. I must have given her some kind of reaction when she mentioned the men in my life. It was so obvious. What she has is a talent for reading people, probably from decades of practice.

The bartender set the tall drink in front of Heather. She took a large gulp. *Whoa, too strong.* But the combination of ice and cold liquid cooled her emotions.

I wonder what was in the gilded book she didn't want me to see?

As she ruminated, the fingers on her left hand opened to reveal the pin feather still in her palm. What was it doing there? She'd seen it float out. Or maybe she'd imagined it. In any case, she didn't want the thing, so she brushed it out of her hand onto the bar.

"She's amazing, isn't she?" Sandos Vendeglo's voice sliced into her thoughts.

Heather hadn't heard him creep up from behind. "Hi, Sandy."

He slid onto the next stool. "Hello, beautiful."

I hate to be addressed that way.

His thick finger motioned toward the tiny plume. "I see she gave you one of her feathers."

"She probably hands one to everyone who comes in the studio. I don't believe a thing she says, and I told her as much, in no uncertain terms."

Sandy's dark eyes narrowed. "Not a smart thing to do." He glanced from side to side and leaned in closer. "She has powers. She knows things."

Heather closed her eyes in disgust. "Don't tell me the woman's gotten to you, too."

He plucked the swizzle stick from his drink and rolled it between his fingers, revealing part of the snake tattoo on his arm. It matched the snake on the page in the gilded book she'd just seen in Madam's studio.

He's definitely a follower.

Sandy tossed the stick on the counter. "I have to admit, she's come up with some pretty accurate stuff. And her guidance has helped me in many other ways."

Heather gave him a side glance. "It seems to me, the woman pushes for a reaction, reads whatever she can into it, and then charges you for it."

"If you're such a non-believer, why did you visit her?"

"I had to see what the Madam was all about for my own peace of mind. I don't want that charlatan fleecing my aunt because Julia's convinced some old crone has put a curse on her."

Heather took another gulp of her drink, easing the tension in her shoulders. She shouldn't be drinking, since she was driving. But Madam Z could infuriate Mother Theresa.

The wrinkles around Sandy's eyes tightened. "The madam's exceptional at getting rid of unwanted things."

I can imagine. "How do you suppose she does it?"

Before Sandy could answer, Julia flung the front door open and ran up to the bar, her red hair as wild as the look in her eyes. She pulled Heather off the bar stool. "Come on. We have to get to the pawn shop before it closes!"

Chapter 14

HEATHER pulled her rental car up to the front of the pawn shop just as the indoor lights dimmed. Julia jumped out of the still moving vehicle and yelled, "Wait! Don't close yet!" She pushed against the door as the clerk turned the key in the lock.

"Sorry," he yelled through the glass.

"You're going to be much sorrier if you don't open up!" She tapped on the glass with her fingernails. Not getting a reply, she pounded on it with both fists. "You'll find out what sorry really means if you don't open this door!"

Heather turned off the engine and leapt out of the driver's seat. "Stop it. You'll break the glass."

"I hope it does break." She continued to pound and yell. "Then they'll have to open." Julia's crimson face matched her fiery red hair and told Heather she meant every word. What had Madam Z said to her to make her this crazy?

A squad car pulled up in front of the shop, and Officer Henderson got out.

"What's the trouble?"

Julia dropped her hands to her sides. "I'm glad you're here. Would you please make the store owner open up for me?"

The officer glanced from Julia to Heather. "Will one of you tell me what this is about?"

"It's simple," Julia said. "I need to retrieve something from the pawn shop. And I need it tonight."

"Can't you wait until tomorrow when they reopen?"

"No. It has to be tonight. It's an emergency!"

Officer Henderson pushed his hat back on his head and rested his hands on his hips. "What kind of emergency?"

"It's personal." Julia motioned to the door. "Now do your job."

The officer huffed as if he'd had enough of this conversation. "It's not my job to make the owner open the shop for you, so if you won't tell me why, I'm leaving." He sauntered off to his quad car, slid into the driver's seat, and sat there.

Heather put an arm around Julia's tense shoulders. "We might as well leave. The officer's gonna wait in his car until we do."

Julia's kohl-lined eyes squinted. "You might be right."

A silent moment later, Julia's eye-lids fluttered. A sure sign she was trying to come up with an idea. "There are other ways."

"What other ways? And what is it you need so urgently?"

"My red stiletto sandals." Julia scrunched her face to the window and pointed. "They were right there, next to that beaded evening bag. I could view them from the front window. And now they're gone."

"Maybe he moved them?"

"Or maybe he sold them."

"He can't sell them as long as you have your pawn ticket, right?"

"Well, I didn't exactly pawn them. I sold them to him, but I still have my receipt."

"You can't redeem your shoes if he's sold them to someone else."

Julia motioned toward the street with her thumb, indicating the officer was watching them. "Let's move on." She headed to the parking lot at the back of the store. Heather had to run to keep up.

"The reason I have to get them back is because they're part of the ritual."

Out of breath, Heather stopped her aunt. "What ritual?"

"The ritual I have to do tonight to rid myself of the crone's curse. Don't you understand? I was wearing them when the curse was put on me. So I have to wear them in order for it to be taken off. And it has to be tonight. The full moon is already waning."

So that's what Madam Z told her. It sounded crazy, like the woman herself.

Julia waited at the back door of the pawn shop as the owner locked up to leave. "I have to talk to you."

He turned and stiffened. "I'm not going to open the store up."

Julia's flat-lined lips turned into an ingratiating smile. "I only want to ask you a question."

He scratched his balding head and gave her a side glance. "What do you want to know?"

"I didn't see my red stilettos in the front window. Did you move them?"

"No. I sold them this morning."

"To whom?"

His beady eyes narrowed. "Why should I tell you?"

"I couldn't help wondering who the fortunate woman was." Julia batted her short eyelashes at him. "You can trust me. We've done a lot of business."

"Yeah, we have. Pardon me if I'm skeptical, but you were involved in her fa... um that murder case last week. And trust has to be earned. Now if you'll excuse me. I'm late for dinner." He turned on his heel and headed toward a black SUV in the parking lot.

"Oh no. Not Krystal Stamos." Heather put a hand over her stomach, a sudden case of nausea.

Julia's shoulders dropped as her hands flopped to her sides. "We'll have to find out where she lives. Call the guy she was engaged to for me, will ya?"

"Forget it. I'm not asking Chad. He'll want to know why I need it. And what do I tell him?"

"Okay. Then I'll ask someone else."

One call to Christine Talan had Julia tapping Krystal's address into the car's navigation system. Heather crossed her arms. "This is not good."

"As far as I can see, we have only two options. It's either ask to buy them back or steal them from her closet. It's your choice."

Heather started the car. One of these days, one of her aunt's hair-brained ideas was going to get her into more trouble than they could handle. She was hoping to avoid the rude, former underwear model while she was living here. "I doubt if she'll welcome us with open arms. She and I don't exactly like each other. We each made it abundantly clear the last time we met."

"So, we'll buy her a cake at the bakery and take it over as a peace offering."

Heather frowned. *This should be fun.*

Chapter 15

FOR some reason, Aunt Julia always thought buying someone a cake would smooth out any resentments or hard feelings, and everything would be happiness and light. She was in for an eye-opening experience.

"Being an underwear model, Krystal's probably on a perpetual diet," Heather said. "I doubt she'd welcome a cake."

Julia patted a few stands of hair back in place. "Don't be silly. Women like her are always hungry. She'll eat it. Maybe not in front of us, but she'll eventually eat it. Especially if she's living alone. You mark my words."

After stopping at the bakery, Heather pulled her rental into the driveway of the two-story, white brick, Ionic-columned house with four equally white Greek figurines adorning the front lawn.

Julia got out and popped a tiny peppermint into her mouth. "Wow! Isn't this lovely?"

Not exactly her taste, but Heather had to admit, it appeared clean and well-kept.

"If Nikkos and I had married, all this would be mine." Julia let out a long, slow sigh.

Heather slid out of the driver's seat as Julia knocked on the front door. She'd stay in the background and let her aunt do the talking.

After a few moments, the Greek goddess herself opened the door, wearing a short black sheath the same color as her smooth, waist-length hair. Her height enhanced by the shocking sight of Aunt Julia's red stiletto sandals.

Krystal's smoky-hued gaze studied them a moment. "What do you want?"

Julia put on a sincere-looking grin and shoved the cake box into Krystal's hands.

"We want you go have this cake with our heartfelt condolences on the death of your father."

Krystal's ruby lips turned up into a smile that never made it to her eyes. "How thoughtful."

"May we come in?" Julia pushed her way into the living room. Heather followed.

Krystal put the cake box on the clear glass cocktail table. "I suppose I should be grateful to you for your help in finding my father's killer."

"All in a day's work." Julia sounded blasé, when if fact, it was anything but blasé.

Krystal made her way to a polished oak cabinet. "It's been a rough day. I could use a drink." The dark-tinged circles under her eyes, where the cover cream had been wiped off, were a giveaway. "Anyone else?"

Julia nodded. "Yes, I'll have a small brandy."

"Nothing for me," Heather said. "I'm driving."

With a twist of a key, the cabinet opened into a mini bar. Krystal poured clear liquid into a martini glass from a frosted decanter for herself and a shot of brandy into a snifter she handed to Julia.

"There's something I'd like to talk to you about." Julia said.

Krystal took a sip of her cocktail. "What?"

"It's about your father. He stole something from me."

Krystal's back straightened. She raised her perfect, salon-tweezed eyebrows and sucked in a short breath of surprise. "What are you talking about?"

"It's a racing ticket, dated May 19th of this year, for the last race of the day."

Heather cringed. *Is she still harping about her lost ticket?*

There was an awkward silence as Krystal took another gulp of her drink. "I deeply resent your accusation. My father was a legitimate business man."

"Julia downed her brandy in one gulp, set her glass on the coffee table, and stood. "Then do you mind if I search his desk?"

Krystal pointed to the door. "Get out!"

"You want us to leave?" Julia sounded surprised. "But we were just getting acquainted. How about having a piece of the chocolate cake I brought?"

Krystal ran a hand along her slim thigh. "Do I look like I eat sweets?"

Julia tossed her head back and laughed.

Krystal's face became bright red and she stamped her foot. "Out, right now. Or I'll call the police and have them throw you out." She scrolled through her cell phone.

"We were leaving anyway." Julia motioned to Heather with her hand. "If you're not going to eat his cake, I'll take it back."

Julia headed for the cocktail table and crashed into Krystal, who's gaze had been fixed on her cell phone.

Krystal tumbled backward, caught her foot on the marble table leg, and landed on the white carpet with a light thud, before letting out a loud yelp.

"Are you hurt?" Julia rushed to her side. "You weren't looking where you were going."

"You tripped me, you clumsy oaf!" Krystal grabbed her ankle. "Ow! Feels like it might be broken."

"Let me take a look." Julia moved closer. "I once worked in a vet's office."

Krystal pulled her ankle back as tears filled her eyes. "Don't touch it!"

Julia waved a hand to indicate she understood. "At least let me take off your shoes."

She eased both stilettos off as Krystal winced in pain. Julia waved one of the shoes in her face. "It wasn't my fault you fell. It's these shoes."

"I've worn stiletto sandals before with no problem."

"No. I mean it's these particular shoes. An old crone put a curse on them, and whoever wears the stilettos will carry *the shroud of death* on her shoulders."

Krystal's face deteriorated into dozens of tiny creases. "I don't believe in curses."

Julia wagged a finger at her. "You better believe in this one, because I was wearing these when she spit on them."

"Eeewww!" Krystal gazed at the shoe. "Those were *your* shoes?"

"Do you want to be responsible for people dying in this town?"

"Ridiculous." Krystal bit her bottom lip and winced, as she rubbed her ankle.

Julia glanced at Heather with a sly smile, like she knew she had the upper hand. "I'll be glad to take these shoes off your hands. You probably won't want them anymore."

"I certainly don't want to wear an old lady's castoffs with some crone's spit on them."

Julia grinned. "I don't blame you." Then her lips cast down into a frown. "Who are you calling old?" She rushed to the end table and fumbled with the cake box as Krystal texted a message on her cell phone.

"Come on, Heather, we're leaving."

On the drive back, a silent Julia sat in the passenger's seat clutching the box.

"All the trouble you caused, and you didn't get your shoes back."

"I wouldn't say that." Julia opened the cover of the box.

Heather hit the brakes. "Now we'll have to turn around and take those shoes right back."

"We can't. Krystal's probably on her way to the emergency room at the hospital to get her ankle checked out. Besides, she as much as admitted she didn't want to wear them anymore. So what difference does it make? If she wants the shoes back, she knows where to find me."

"I can't believe it. Madam Z has turned you into a thief."

"I'm not stealing. I'm borrowing." Julia raised a finger. "There's a difference."

"You might have permanently injured Krystal." Not that she cared, but she had to ask. "Did you stage her accident?"

"Of course not. It just turned out to be a fortuitous coincidence."

Why don't I believe you? "So, what's next on your agenda?"

"Drop me off at Christine's house. You needn't stay. Chris said she'd drive me home."

"If you say so." *But where else is she going to drive you?*

Chapter 16

A UNT Julia popped a tiny peppermint into her mouth as Heather pulled into the Talan's drive. She stepped out of the car. "See you at home."

There could only be two reasons why her aunt wanted to be alone with Christine. One was to carry out an idiotic ritual to rid herself of the curse, and the other was to concoct some crazy scheme to investigate Esther Quinn's murder.

Heather backed her car out of the driveway and pulled around to park on the other side of the street. This way she'd be in a better position to follow Christine's car, in case they decided to go someplace risky tonight.

As she waited, Heather checked her cell phone for emails but kept going back to the one from her "so-called" office friend. She might be out of favor with her former clients and a non-existent competitor to her previous boss, but she wasn't out of the advertising game yet. She'd find other clients and work under the radar until she could reestablish herself as a reliable business partner, no matter how long it took.

I'll just have to find a different approach to advertising. But it was hard to come up with anything at the moment. There were too many other things on her mind.

A black Lexus turned the corner. Dusk had descended on the town, but it was still light enough to see Ashley in the passenger's seat. Miklos was driving.

Heather ducked out of sight behind the steering wheel. *Coming back from their date so soon? Or maybe they stopped to pick something up.* She craned her neck to see. Miklos carried Ashley through the front door. He didn't come back out.

I wonder if Chad's in there? His car isn't in the drive-way. It might be in the garage. She was tempted to call and talk to him about how the situation with her aunt had escalated. After considering it for a few moments, she tapped his name on her contact list. His voicemail answered.

"Hi, it's Heather. If you're still interested in what the mumbo-jumbo is about, call me." *That should get his attention.*

Heather yawned as she sat in her car, waiting. Time dragged. Heaviness tugged at her eyelids. She shut her eyes to rest them for a moment and dozed off.

A knock on the window.

Her insides jumped, and she blinked into the darkness. "What?"

Chad's face appeared in the front windshield. Heart pounding, she rolled down her driver's side window.

He leaned in. "I was about to call you back when I saw your car parked out here. Are you stalking me?"

"Oh, God, no."

"Then what are you doing here?"

Heather rubbed her eyes, still heavy with sleep. "It has to do with my aunt, and... it's a long story."

"Why don't you come in. We can discuss it over coffee."

"I believe your sister and Miklos are in the house."

"Oh yeah." Chad's lips frowned. "The date."

"You don't sound pleased."

"Well, Miklos is so..."

Insincere. "You don't have to say it. I'm familiar with his kind. But he seems genuinely fond of Ashley."

"I just don't want to see her hurt again."

"Shouldn't it be up to Ashley? She is an adult."

"You're right." He glanced over his right shoulder. "Sit tight. I'll be back in a minute." Chad moved away from her car and jogged to his garage.

Heather checked her face in the rear-view mirror, wiping away the residue of black liner from under her eyes, then she combed her long auburn hair with her fingers, giving it a slightly messy but fashionable look.

A few moments later, he came out carrying a pint-sized, white bag. Then he walked around to open her passenger's side door.

"Mind if I get in? My neck's getting stiff from talking to you through the window."

"Sure. Make yourself comfortable. Or as comfortable as you can in the front seat of a car."

He opened the bag. "Would you like some?"

She glanced down into it. Chunks of dark chocolate fudge with walnuts filled it to the top. They were her favorite, but he knew that from their first meeting at the *Fudge Shop* in town last week.

"Thanks. I need this right now." She reached inside and picked out a piece. "You're spoiling me. I don't buy these for myself because, if I did, I'd eat the entire contents of the bag in one sitting."

He grabbed a chunk. "I've often done that. It's one of my guilty pleasures."

A mellow feeling washed over her. *When he puts on that boyish charm, he could easily sweep me off my feet. So why doesn't he?*

Chad put the bag on the console between them. "Now, tell me all about the mumbo-jumbo. For a moment, I thought you actually believed in evil spirits."

His voice was soft and his breath sweet with the faint scent of fudge. All at once, she was painfully aware of his nearness, bare inches from the dark stubble that peppered his jaw. Her heart pounded in her ears.

"Huh?" *Pull yourself together.* "I mean, I do believe there's evil in the world, but I don't think it's in the form of spirits."

"I agree." He sniffed, then turned his head away, and rolled the window half-way down. "It's a warm night."

What is he smelling? She took a quick whiff of her sleeve while trying to look inconspicuous. A faint scent of Jack's aftershave still lingered on her clothes. She pretended not to notice.

"I, um... I." She closed her eyes. *Focus!* "I had a talk with Madam Z. I hate to see anyone taken advantage of by a charlatan. My aunt's at the stage now where she won't make a move without talking to her first. And she's being charged for the privilege. I told the woman what I thought of her and her ideologies."

Chad narrowed his eyes. In the dark, his face took on an eerie glow from the reflection of the dim street lamp. "It's one thing to not believe in what she says or does, but telling her off is another. You have to remember, she's lived in this town her entire life. The woman has connections and she knows a lot about people."

"Does that give her some kind of power over them?"

"Not exactly. More like a great deal of influence with people who are in power."

"Sandy said the same thing."

"Sandos Vendeglo? When did you talk to him?"

"After I saw Madam Z."

"Was he in your car at the time?"

"No."

He sniffed. "I thought I..."

He couldn't possibly imagine I'd have anything to do with Sandos.

Chad folded his arms in front of his chest. "Never mind. Continue with your story."

She swallowed her last mouthful of fudge. "Madam Z told my aunt she needed to wear the red stiletto sandals when she did her curse purging ritual tonight. As it turned out, my aunt had sold them to the pawn broker in town last week. But he'd resold them."

"Don't tell me your aunt tried to get them back?"

"Tried and succeeded."

"So, she got what she wanted."

"Yes, through trickery and deceit." *Not to mention nearly breaking your ex's ankle to do it.*

They sat in a moment of uncomfortable silence as he studied her face. *I can only imagine what he must be thinking of us.*

"You never told me why you're out here."

Heather leaned back in her seat. "My aunt had me take her back to Christine's after she 'acquired' the shoes. I wanted to follow them in case the ladies did something dangerous tonight."

A moment later, Christine's car backed out of her driveway and headed toward town.

"And they're off." Heather started her engine. Putting her car in drive, she said, "Unless you want to follow my aunt around all night, you might want to get out."

Chapter 17

"Not on your life." Chad buckled his seatbelt. "I wouldn't miss this for the world."

"I'm a little perturbed you find my aunt's feeble attempts at sleuthing amusing."

"Not amused, concerned. Especially when they include my friend and neighbor when her husband's out of town."

It's comforting to know he's as worried about them as I am. Heather followed Christine's car at a discreet distance all the way to the police station parking lot.

"This is the last place I would have guessed my aunt wanted to go."

"I thought she and Detective Lindsey were pretty cozy these days."

"She hasn't said anything to me about it."

"Then maybe she's telling him she and Christine will be doing some investigating on their own."

She wouldn't tell him anything. "More like she's trying to squirm a few facts about Esther's murder out of *him.*"

Chad stretched his arms over his head. "If you're satisfied your aunt's safe, would you mind driving me home?"

"Guess you think I'm pretty silly for chasing her all over town."

"Not at all. I can see why you'd want to keep an eye on her after the murder last week."

The one you and I solved together. Heather circled the parking lot and headed toward town. After driving a couple of miles, she stopped near the front of his house.

Don't sit here like a bump on a log, say something! "Can I walk you to your door?" *That sounded juvenile.*

His eyebrows rose. "How can I pass up an invitation like that?"

After a slow stroll up the driveway, they finally reached the front of the house. She turned to face him. "I guess this is goodnight."

He gazed into her eyes. "I guess it is. And in case I forgot to mention it, you look lovely in the moonlight."

She couldn't look away. His words grazed her heart as heat rose to her cheeks. Then his gaze lowered to her lips. A flutter in her stomach told her a kiss was imminent.

She waited, but something behind her had taken his focus away.

What's he looking at? She turned around. A pale light in the distance increased intensity by the minute as plumes of white smoke trailed skyward.

Chad's cell buzzed. He checked the screen. "There's a fire in a warehouse behind the police station. Sorry. I have to leave. I'm an alternate on the Volunteer Fire Brigade."

Of course he is. And just as we were getting somewhere.

Heather got back in her car and followed him. The fire engine sirens added to her panicked thoughts. A sick, tightening knot twisted her gut. *Christine and my aunt were headed in that direction. Could they be involved? What is Julia not telling me?*

***

Parking anywhere near the fire was impossible. Heather drove to the next block and parked in front of *The Club Car Diner.*

The gray-haired proprietor of the glorified hot dog stand watched the fire though binoculars.

"Excuse me. I'd like a cup of coffee, please."

The elderly man took the binoculars down and placed them on the counter. "Sure, your coffee'll be right up."

Smoke caught in her throat. She waved a hand in front of her face to waft it away without much success. "What was in the warehouse?"

The man turned around. "Old newspapers. The building used to be a recycling center. It should have been torn down years ago."

She picked up the binoculars. "Can I borrow these a minute?"

"Help yourself."

She took another breath. The smoke clung to her lungs, and she coughed to clear them. Raising the binoculars, she gazed all around the grounds surrounding the blazing building. If her aunt was in the crowd somewhere, she'd be hard to find.

With the firefighters and policemen milling around, all the spectators, and the enormous billows of smoke covering everything in a dense fog, it was difficult to make out individual faces.

Something moved on the edge of the field. Something which gradually took form and shape in the moonlight. A lone person ducked and weaved through the thick, foot-high grass, past the police station, into the lighted parking lot jammed with cars, and then out into the street.

An SUV, resembling Christine's, pulled up alongside the figure. The now visible woman with wild red hair slipped into the passenger's side. A moment later, the SUV sped off in the direction of town.

What was Aunt Julia doing in that field?

Heather paid for her coffee and gave the binoculars back. "Thanks."

A heavy hand tapped her shoulder. She twitched, and the cover on her coffee cup saved the liquid from splashing out. She hadn't noticed anyone else around, but then her mind had been focused on her aunt.

"What are you doin' here all by your lonesome?" Sandy Vendeglo stood beside her, the muscles on his broad chest straining the fabric of his white tee shirt with the restaurant's logo printed across it.

"I'm watching the fire from a safe distance."

"Yeah, me too. There's not much to do in this town. This is as exiting as things get around here."

"I wouldn't know."

He grinned. "I forgot you haven't been in town long."

"I'm surprised you're not at the restaurant tonight."

"We close early on Wednesdays. Not much business in the middle of the week. But I'm there every other night until ten, and on the weekends till eleven."

"Sounds like you put a lot of work into your business."

"We're proud of it. The restaurant was passed down to us from our parents and their parents before them. Granddad opened it in 1947, when this town was starting out."

Heather took a cautious sip of coffee. "You must love the place."

"It's our home. The only one I've ever known. I'd be lost without the restaurant."

"Does your brother feel the same?"

"Why wouldn't he?"

At a loss for words, Heather changed the subject. "I noticed Miklos is working on putting out the fire. I'm surprised you're not with the Fire Brigade. They could use your help."

His eyes dimmed. "That's my brother's thing. He only joined the Brigade yesterday. He's trying to win points with Ashley." Sandy grumbled. "As if he's got a chance to marry into *that* family."

What does that *mean?* She raised an eyebrow. "Ashley seems to like him."

"Yeah, what's not to like about my brother? But don't judge me. I do a lot of other things for this town."

Seems a little full of himself. "I'm not judging you. How can I? You're practically a stranger."

He leaned in closer, his cheek nearly touching hers. "Maybe we can change that."

Uh oh. Heat rose to her face, and it wasn't from the fire.

She turned to view the flames licking the sky, as smoke billowed out of the blazing inferno. "Do you know who owns the warehouse?"

"Why? You got some kind of interest in it?"

"Just curious."

"It'll be on the local news tonight." He stepped in front of her. "Now why don't we resume the subject of you getting to know me better."

My cue to leave. She faked a coughing fit, not hard to do with the smell of smoke in the air. "I have to move away from here. The smoke's getting to me."

"Can I drive you home?"

"No. I have my car." *Thank goodness.* "But it was kind of you to offer."

She rushed to get in and drove home. It was time to confront her aunt.

Chapter 18

No lights were on in the apartment. The living room was lit by a half dozen candles set in a circle on the cocktail table surrounding a silver pentacle.

What's going on? "Aunt Julia, where are you?"

No answer, but her hair dryer hummed from inside the bathroom.

She flipped on the lights in the kitchen and set her coffee cup on the counter. The toe of a soiled red stiletto sandal stuck out of a sheet of crumbled newspaper on the floor near the sink. *This doesn't look good.*

Heather did a quick search though all the drawers for the television remote. Highlights of the blaze were sure to be on the local news station. Maybe some official found out what started it. Drawer after drawer yielded nothing. Most were empty, except for a few junk items Chad had told her his grandfather liked to collect.

She slipped off her shoes and plopped on the living room sofa to check her phone for news of the fire.

A few minutes later, Julia stepped out of the bathroom wearing her silk, blue peacock feather print robe.

Heather caught up to her at the door. "Washed your hair, I see."

Julia jumped "Oh, you're home."

"Yeah, I just got here." Heather raised an eyebrow and pointed to the living room. "What's that all about?"

"Just a precaution." Julia leaned toward her niece and sniffed. "Smells like you were at the fire too. Everybody in town was there. What a crowd."

"Why don't you tell me why *you* were there."

"Curiosity."

"That couldn't be the only reason. Why were you really there?"

Julia opened and slammed each kitchen cabinet door. "We got any whiskey?"

"Yes, but why do you need a bracer to tell me why you were at the fire?"

Julia drummed her fingers on the counter. "Will you please find the whiskey. Have some yourself—might make what I have to say go down a little easier."

Heather's stomach tightened. "Aunt Julia, you're scaring me." She grabbed the bottle from the bottom cabinet, poured out two fingers each in a couple of juice glasses, and handed one to her aunt.

Julia gulped hers down. "You're going to laugh when I tell you what happened."

Heather's heart sank. "I hope so."

"Well, it's like this..." Julia licked her lips. "When I consulted Madam Z tonight, she gave me another ritual. This was supposed to be the next step in obliterating the curse. If I did it *perfectly*."

"Uh huh." Heather took a sip of whiskey to steady her nerves. "What did she instruct you to do?"

"She gave me a bunch of twigs. Well, they weren't only twigs. They were a bundle of herbs, dried flowers, tree bark, and some other stuff she said contained mystical powers. Then she explained where I was to go."

Heather took another sip of her drink and shuddered. *Can't wait to hear the rest.*

Julia toyed with the empty glass in her hand. "After I got the stilettos back, and you dropped me off at Christine's, I put the shoes on, and we checked out the area where Madam Z told me to do the ritual. Chris showed me where it was on a local map, because I had to be in the perfect place at precisely the right time, or it wouldn't work. You understand?"

Heather wiped perspiration from her forehead. *Must be the whiskey.* "I'm beginning to get the drift."

Julia paced, head down, arms folded. "Before we left, I wrote my wish on a large piece of brown wrapping paper, which Christine had saved from a package she'd received earlier that day. I wrapped the paper around the huge bundle, twisting it closed at both ends. Once I got to the exact place I was directed to be, I checked my watch, and the time was right, so I lit the paper while chanting: *This curse has been—*"

Heather put a hand up to stop her. "Skip the chant, please."

"After I finished reciting it the first time, the paper was burning pretty well. I could smell the fragrant flowers and herbs and spices. So I took a deep breath to inhale their clearing abilities and chanted for the second time while staring at the night sky. It was eerily dark out. I was mesmerized by the nearly full moon and the stars for a few moments, and then the smoke made me dizzy, so I closed my eyes.

When I opened them, some dried leaves under the bundle had caught fire. And then the wind picked up. The leaves, along with the flaming paper, flew up and into a broken warehouse window before I could catch them." Julia shook a finger. "And believe me, I did my best. Those darn shoes. The heels kept sinking into the soft dirt. The next thing I knew, the building was on fire. Whatever was in there must have been extremely flammable."

Heather dragged her hands over her face. "It was a paper recycling warehouse."

"That explains it."

"Then what did you do?"

"I called Christine. She notified the fire department, and after a while, she picked me up and drove me home."

Heather chugged what was left in her glass. She needed something to wash down this fantastic story. "Now Madam Z has you committing arson."

Julia put a calming hand on Heather's shoulder. "It's no use blaming her. It wasn't a deliberate act."

"You have to tell the police what happened."

"I will..." Julia's gaze darted to the ceiling. "If I have to."

"Of *course* you have to."

Julia's lips flat-lined. "Right now I'm in enough trouble. Do you want me to go to prison for life?"

"Well, no, but—"

"For goodness sake, it was an accident. No one got hurt. That old building was probably insured for more money than it's worth." Julia waved her hands in the air. "I don't want to talk about it anymore tonight. I'm going to bed. I have to be up early. The *Willows Retirement Village* bus is picking me up downstairs at 8:00 a.m."

"This conversation's not over," Heather called after her aunt as Julia scurried to her room and slammed the door.

Chapter 19

HEATHER checked the drawers for the television remote once again. Nothing. It would be ideal if she had the latest news update on the fire.

There was no information on her computer either, so she showered and washed her long, auburn hair. As she blow dried it, she debated whether or not to go to the police with the information about her aunt. Should she involve herself or stay out of it and count on her aunt to do the right thing?

The results of the fire department's investigation might show the fire was accidental. Then there would be no need to tell anyone. If she thought about it in those terms, at least she'd be able to sleep tonight. But every time she closed her eyes, visions of the fire, and her aunt running away, played over and over.

At 2:00 am, she'd had enough. She got out of bed for some warm milk. Or maybe a dull book to read.

In the kitchen, her aunt stood at the sink washing something in the dark. The water wasn't running, but Julia's hands were busy scrubbing an imaginary object.

Heather studied her for a few moments. "What are you doing?"

Julia continued to scrub and rinse. "I have to get these stilettos clean. Krystal will never forgive me if she sees them with all this dirt caked on."

Heather observed one of the soiled shoes still on the floor a few feet away from where Julia stood. What did her aunt do with the other? She peered into the sink. No shoe in there.

She'd look for the other shoe tomorrow. Right now, she'd better get her aunt back to her room before she went to Krystal's house to return a pair of imaginary sandals.

"Krystal said she wasn't going to wear them anymore," Heather said. "So why don't you leave the shoes and go back to bed. Remember, you have an early morning tomorrow."

Julia continued scrubbing. "I should get them back to her tonight."

"I'll finish cleaning the shoes and take them back for you."

Julia went through the motions of turning off the imaginary water, and then she wiped her hands on an imaginary kitchen towel. "You're a good niece."

Obviously satisfied with Heather's offer, Julia headed back to her room.

Heather could only shake her head. *She's sleepwalking again.*

***

In the morning, Heather woke at 7:30 a.m. She turned off her alarm and got out of bed to brew a pot of coffee, but from the smell, one had already been brewed.

Julia passed her in the hall. "Oh, you're up. Gotta run. I don't want to be late."

"But the bus won't be here until eight."

"Did I say eight? I meant 7:30."

"We have to talk."

Julia glanced out the living room window. "Not now. The bus is pulling up to the curb. I'll find out what I can about Esther's murder at the retirement village, and we'll talk later." She scurried to the door. "Oh, there's one more thing."

Heather wasn't sure she could handle another thing. "What is it now?"

"I lost the other red shoe last night somewhere in the field. Would you be a doll and find it for me? If Lindsey discovers it first, he'll be sure to connect me to the fire."

"But I thought you and he were—"

Julia raised an eyebrow. "I decline to discuss our so-called relationship." She blew Heather a kiss. "Thanks. I don't know what I'd do without your help."

Heather stared at the front door with her mouth open. This was typical of Aunt Julia, dropping a guilt bomb before running off. It was fortunate she couldn't leave town, or Heather might not see her for *another* five years. Not that *that* would be a terrible thing. And to think, she assured her mom Julia had turned over a new leaf.

It's just like her to lose a shoe. The police probably have the whole area cordoned off. How am I supposed to find it?

Heather burst into the bathroom and splashed cool water on her face as she let everything sink in. "Find the incriminating shoe. Go to the retirement village to see what Aunt Julia's up to. Search for the television remote to keep a visual eye on what's happening in town. For someone without a job, I'm swamped. And working on my job is another thing to add to my 'to-do' list."

She poured herself a cup of freshly brewed coffee and took a sip. Her stomach grumbled. She'd better fortify herself before starting out. *Scrambled eggs and toast would taste great right now.* She pulled out a frying pan.

Parking herself in front of her laptop, she ate breakfast while scrolling for any news about the fire.

Nothing. *Why would there be? This town is so far from anywhere, who'd care except the locals?*

She read her emails and deleted the one from her so-called office friend. It reminded her she'd made some poor decisions, and she didn't need reminding.

Heather dressed in her jeans and a pale green tee shirt, to blend in better with the background of the area she'd be searching. She pulled her shoulder length, auburn hair into a pony tail, and slipped on a pair of sneakers, good enough for stomping around in a wet, ash-filled field on a warm morning.

She ran down the back stairs and jumped into her car. As she pulled into the street, the man in the bomber jacket leaned against the bookstore window, smoking, as if he was waiting for someone or for something to happen.

The tiny hairs on the back of her neck bristled. She should stop and talk to him, but there wasn't time. *I have to find my aunt's shoe before the police discover it.*

Why am I doing this?

"To prove to my mother she's wrong about me being like her sister. I'm not. She'll see how responsible I am when I help Julia get out of this mess."

Chapter 20

BEFORE she drove to the field, Heather stopped at the hotel. She entered the lobby, but no one was manning the front desk.

"Hello, anyone here?"

No answer.

She ducked into the breakfast room to catch a quick glimpse of the news on the television. The weather lady explained the weather today would be in the lower 80s. Partly cloudy and humid with a twenty percent chance of rain.

She chewed her thumbnail, something she hadn't done since grammar school. "Forget the weather. Get to the news."

A bird's eye-view of the warehouse fire came up on the screen as a hand clamped her shoulder. "You're not supposed to be in here. This room is strictly for hotel guests."

Vikki, the desk clerk, smiled. "You're not a guest here anymore."

Heather scrunched her nose. "The fire sirens were blasting all evening, and I wanted to see what the noise was about."

"Didn't you catch it on the news last night?"

"I don't have access to a television at the moment. But I remembered this one was on all morning. So, I came in."

"Nothing to see but a lot of flames and smoke when the old paper recycling warehouse burned."

"Do they know how it started?"

"They're still investigating. But the police speculate it might have been kids playing with fire or a careless smoker."

Not arson? "Thanks for the information."

Heather got into her car and headed toward the police station. She parked on the street, a half block away. No officers came in or out, and no police tape cordoned off the area. But a smoky haze still lingered in the morning air.

Holding a tissue over her nose and mouth, she made her way to the field. The black shell of the burned-out building smoldered under the gloom of dark clouds in the morning sky. The smoke got stronger the nearer she got to the building as she inspected the wet, black ash for the lost shoe.

She covered a quarter of the area in ten minutes, resulting in a few beer cans and several old potato chip bags, and then she stumbled. Light-headedness made it hard to go any farther. She staggered to the parking lot to catch a few breaths of fresher air.

Chad stood next to his car, his eyes wide as she approached. "Hey, what are you doing here?"

Heather hated to lie, but she couldn't tell him the truth.

"I came to see the..." She coughed. "I wanted to find out what..." Another coughing fit racked her chest.

"The air's still lousy out here. Come into the station for a while."

She pinched the bridge of her nose in an attempt to stop the dizziness. "Maybe I will come in for a minute, to get a drink of water."

Chad opened the door. She rushed inside and sucked in a welcomed breath of cool air.

He smiled. "Better?"

She sucked in another deep breath and let it out. "Much."

He motioned toward the far end of the room. "The water cooler's over there."

Heather was familiar with the room, having been here twice before on two unrelated occasions.

"I have a better idea," Chad said. "If you'll wait a few minutes while I sign a statement about last night's fire, I'll take you out for coffee."

She checked her cell phone. *Eleven o'clock.* She had to get back to searching the rest of the field for the other shoe. "Thanks, but I'll have to take a rain check on the coffee. I have something important to do right now."

He smiled. "I'll hold you to that."

I hope so.

She sauntered to the cooler and grabbed a cup of water as he disappeared to the other side of the room. Gulping it down, she rushed toward the door for another quick search. Officer Henderson opened it and came in holding a clear plastic bag containing her aunt's stiletto.

She stopped as heat burned her cheeks. *I can't leave now.*

He stepped back to let her pass. "Hi."

Heather couldn't let him sense she was interested in the shoe. She gave him a quick grin. "Hi, yourself."

"What did we haul your aunt in for now?"

She chuckled, trying to make light of the subject. "Nothing." *At least not yet.* "I came in for a drink of water." She held up the empty paper cup. "And a breath of fresher air. It's still so smoky outside."

"Yeah, it is." He let the door close behind him.

She crushed the cup in her hand. "So, have they found out who, I mean, how the fire started?"

"I can't say at this time." He glanced around. "If you'll excuse me, I have to take this to the..." His head motioned toward the center of the station.

"Nice to see you again."

"You too." He turned and walked over to the group of other police officers crowded around a desk in the middle of the room.

If he's got the shoe, they might be talking about the fire. She eased her way closer to the desk and glanced at the floor on the pretext of searching for a trash can.

Officer Henderson dumped the evidence bag on Detective Lindsey's desk. "The clerk at the Salvation Army store recognized a pair of shoes like this one in the pawn shop. The broker said he'd sold them to..." Henderson stopped talking and turned his head. "Can I help you?"

She didn't think he'd spot her standing behind him. "I'm looking for a waste basket."

He glanced down to one near the desk.

She dropped her paper cup into it. "Thanks."

If only she could hang around and listen, but she already knew what the officer would tell the detective about who the pawn broker sold the shoes to. It was lucky Chad didn't see the evidence bag. She told him Aunt Julia had gotten those shoes back to wear for her curse-ridding ritual.

I'd better call her.

Heather scurried out the door and, holding her breath, made a dash for her car, turned on the engine along with the air conditioner, and grabbed her cell phone.

A few rings, and her aunt answered. "Heather?"

"Sorry, but I was too late. The police already found your shoe."

"Now you have to dump the other one."

"What do you suggest I do with it?"

"Take the cursed thing to Krystal's house and toss it on her property. After all, the shoes belong to her. I only borrowed them."

Heather closed her eyes and put a hand to her forehead. This was too much. "I'm not going to do any such thing. I have to draw the line somewhere."

Julia tsked into the phone. "They do it all the time in the movies. What's the problem?"

"The problem is, we're not in a movie!"

"Minor setback."

There's only one thing to do. "I'm taking the other shoe to the police."

"No please, don't involve the police yet. Wait until the results come back from the investigation, and we'll see. I'd do it myself, but I can't leave. I'm stuck here until 4:30."

"And speaking of where you are, have you found out anything about Esther Kwinn?" Heather was sorry she brought up the subject the minute she said the words.

"I'm working on it. Now will you please dispose of the other shoe before I have a nervous breakdown over this? Please, please, please. Don't make me beg."

The tone of her aunt's voice, near tears, and those sorrowful words—Julia knew how to push her buttons. "I'm not saying I'll do it, but I'll think it over."

"I can always count on you for support. Everything will work out in the end, you'll see. Gotta go. I have a hungry lunch crowd eyeing me like I'm a fried pork chop."

Heather ended the call. *Why does Aunt Julia always get me involved in these things?*

She headed back to her apartment to get the other shoe.

Chapter 21

Get rid of the shoe and lie about seeing it, or take it to the police and have Aunt Julia freak out? *What a decision.*

Heather parked her car in one of the two spaces behind the bookstore. The other was empty. *Chad must still be at the police station. I should have checked the lot for his car. Or gone back inside.*

She climbed the stairs to her apartment, and poured herself a cola. Gulping it down, she kicked at the crumbled newspaper near the sink. The paper flew up and landed near her foot.

"Where's the shoe?" She did a frantic search of the floor. "Was someone here? Did Aunt Julia come back and get it?"

Should she panic or be relieved she didn't have to dispose of it? In either case, the shoe was gone. But her aunt couldn't have taken it—she was busy serving lunch at the retirement village. Then who?

Meow.

The sound came from the direction of her bedroom.

Meow.

"What the heck?" She tiptoed to her room not wanting to scare the cat. Stopping at the door, she stooped down.

Makki stood next to her dresser and gave her a wide, green-eyed, innocent stare.

She had to smile. "How in the world did you get up here?"

Makki sauntered over to her and rubbed his face on her outstretched hand.

Meow.

She petted the soft fur on his back, and then she picked him up. He licked her cheek. She cringed at the sandpaper feel of his tongue. Walking around the room, she checked for possible places he could have gotten in. The cover on the air vent lay pushed aside. *Could he have squeezed in through there?*

"We'd better go downstairs, sweetheart. Ashley gets frantic when she can't find you."

Makki purred and nuzzled his face against her shoulder.

Heather scurried down the stairs and walked into the bookstore cradling the cat in her arms.

Behind the counter, Ashley set down her book. "Where in the world did you find him?"

Heather handed her the cat. "In my apartment."

"Thanks for bringing him back. The last time I saw Makki, he was walking on those top shelves near the ceiling. How did he get in your apartment?"

Heather didn't want Ashley or her brother to be aware of the air vent. At least, not yet. "I have no idea."

Ashley hugged the squirming cat. "Sorry he was such a pest."

"I don't mind having him up there. I love cats. He can visit me any time he likes."

Ashley laughed and kissed Makki's nose. "The next time he does, just call so I won't worry."

"I will."

The door bell tinkled as Chad walked in. He stopped and raised his eyebrows. "Hi. I wasn't expecting to see you here."

"I dropped off your cat. He was in my apartment."

"How did he make his way up there?"

Heather caught Ashley's glance. "We don't know."

"I'll walk you upstairs and check things out."

Ordinarily, she would have been overjoyed to have him come to her apartment. She'd already put the vent cover back on, but if he did search, he might find the shoe.

"This isn't the best time."

"How about if I accompany you to the outside door?"

Why is he being so insistent? She didn't want to be rude. "All right."

He opened the bookstore door and followed her out. Rounding the corner, he halted her with a gentle hand on her shoulder, his voice somber. "When I was at the police station, I overheard a conversation."

She stiffened and turned around to face him.

"I discovered the fire might be arson, but Detective Lindsey doesn't have the particulars yet."

"Once a P.I., always a P.I.?"

His eyes narrowed into a stare. Evidently, he didn't find those words amusing.

"I also caught a glimpse of an evidence bag with a red stiletto and discovered it belongs to Krystal Stamos."

"You've been busy." Heather swallowed hard. "Do they think she started the fire?"

"That would have been difficult, since she was in the emergency room, waiting for an elastic bandage to be wrapped around her sprained ankle at the time."

"I guess it would." *How did he find out? I wouldn't be surprised if she called him for help. That would be just like her.*

"I think we'd better have a little talk about what your aunt did to get those shoes back, and why she was wearing them in the field behind the station last night."

Is he kidding? Heather folded her arms and stood her ground. "I can't tell you."

"Why?"

"Because I have no authority. It's up to my aunt whether or not she wants to admit... I mean, to say anything."

"We both know she was there, and you told me she got the shoes back. If you let me in on the details, maybe we can help your aunt before she's picked up by the police for questioning."

They could use Chad's help right now, but Heather couldn't betray her aunt's trust, not if she ever wanted to face her again.

"My aunt's been questioned by the police before. She can hold her own against anything Detective Lindsey could possibly throw at her. And I'll be there for support."

"Family loyalty is one of the things I admire about you." Chad walked ahead of her to the street door and opened it. "Did you ever find the television remote?"

That's an abrupt subject change. "No, I haven't had a chance to look for it."

His cell phone chimed. He glanced at the screen and put it back in his pocket. "Why don't you go to the attic now? I'll meet you there in a few minutes." He motioned toward the parking area. "Via the back stairs."

"I um..."

"Unless you're too busy."

Better get this over with. "No, I'm free." She could always search for the shoe later. But it seemed like a moot point since the police already had the other one.

Heather made her way to the attic. She opened both windows half way for ventilation. A stiff breeze blew in, scattering dust particles into the air, millions visible in the sun's rays.

She lingered in the middle of the room and studied the banker's boxes stacked three high, one of them labeled, *Granddad's Junk*. Others were labeled *clothes* and *personal belongings*.

Heather wandered over to the other side of the room where an old oak, roll top desk stood. She'd admired it the last few times she'd been up here but hadn't gotten the chance to inspect it. She grabbed the handles. Footsteps on the stairs curbed the urge to open it.

Chad stood at the door. "Great desk, isn't it?"

She snatched her hands away. "Yes, it is. It's almost exactly like the one my Uncle Winston has in his den."

"We have a larger version in our library at the house."

There's a library in his house?

"The one at home was my dad's desk, but since he's moved to Palm Springs, it stands empty," Chad said.

"Is your mom with him?"

"No. My mom passed away. My dad couldn't cope with the house without her there, so he moved out."

"I'm sorry for your loss." Another standard statement, but the best she could come up with at the moment. Getting away from the subject, she rubbed her fingers over the brass catch. "My uncle's desk has a lock similar to this one."

Heather had always been fascinated by that roll-top, mostly because her uncle's desk was always locked. He told her it was because the family secrets were kept there. *I wonder if the Willows family has secrets too.*

Chapter 22

CHAD walked over to the banker's boxes and brought the one labeled "junk" down. He motioned to Heather. "Dig in. We shouldn't have too much trouble finding a TV remote if it's in here."

The box was filled to the top with odd shaped plastic pieces, used bicycle pedals, metal rings, out-of-date radio and television parts, and unidentifiable objects.

It didn't take long to reach the bottom of the box.

"I found it!" Chad held it out to her.

"Thanks. My aunt will be glad to watch her programs again." *And I can watch the local news.*

"You'd do almost anything for your aunt, wouldn't you?"

"I would."

Chad had a warm smile on his face, like he understood. "Are you finished using the attic?" He asked.

She'd taken all her clothes back to her apartment, so there was no need to be up here any longer. "I am."

"Then I guess we're finished up here. Would you mind closing the windows while I put this junk back in the box?"

Heather closed and locked the windows. Then she stooped down to where some of the junk was still piled on the floor. "I'll help."

She picked up as many odd-shaped plastic pieces as she could hold. For a moment, she was like a juggler doing a balancing act. Finally, they all fell out of her hands. She tried to grab them in mid-air and push them toward the box, but instead of going in, they scattered.

Heather stooped down to pick them up, just as Chad did. They collided and both tumbled to the floor.

"Are you hurt?" He asked as he rubbed his elbow.

"No. Except for a little bump on my knee."

A smile broke on Chad's lips. "Is there anything else you'd like to help me with?"

She had to smile too. "This is so typical of the way my life's been going."

He hovered over her and lifted her chin. "Would you like to talk about it?"

Oh boy, would I. The sincerity in his sparkling blue eyes tugged at the heartfelt feelings she had for him. Why did he have to be so handsome? In that instant, she was ready to tell him everything.

A long, slow breath later, she opened her mouth to speak. Then a thought struck her like a slap. *He wants me to tell him about my aunt so he can go to the police with the information. Julia was right. You can't trust men.*

"Actually, I wouldn't."

Heather scooped up the rest of the pieces from the floor and tossed them into the box. "That's everything." She rubbed her hands together to brush off the dust. "I'll be going now." She handed him the door key.

Heather headed back to her apartment with Chad following close behind. Opening the back door, she turned to face him.

"Thanks for finding the remote."

"You're welcome."

She squeezed in and closed the door behind her. *I must seem rude, but I need to find that other shoe.*

He knocked on the door, and she peeked out.

"Would you like to come down to the store for some iced tea?" Chad smiled. "My sister keeps a pitcher in the back room refrigerator."

"Not right now. I'm leaving for the retirement village."

"Which reminds me. There are a dozen or so books we're donating to their library. Would you mind taking them with you?"

"Not at all." *It'll give me an excuse to be there.* "I'll come down in about ten minutes."

Heather put the remote device next to the flat screen television and did a quick search of her apartment for the shoe. "Where could Makki have hidden it?"

She walked into the bedroom and knelt to check under the bed. Voices came up from the floor vent. She put her hand on the vent to close it but hesitated. *This is absolutely the last time I'm going to listen.*

A refrigerator door opened and closed. "Where have you been?" Ashley asked as glasses clinked.

"In the attic with Heather. We were sifting through Grandfather's junk for the television remote."

"You were gone quite a while. What else were you two doing up there?" Ashley's voice teased.

"Nothing," Chad said in annoyed tone. "But there might be something strange going on with Heather."

"What do you mean?"

A pause as footsteps crossed the floor. "She always has an excuse for not letting me into the apartment. When we were in the attic, I could swear I smelled the vague, but distinct, odor of men's aftershave, the same after-shave I smelled in her car, which leads me to believe she may have been hiding a man up there."

Heather let out a squeak. She clapped a hand over her mouth to stifle anymore noises that might escape.

Ashley laughed in a high pitched, melodious tone. "That's too funny. Your P.I. brain has gotten the better of you."

Heather closed the vent and sat up with a grin. "This would be insanely humorous, if it wasn't so disturbing. *After this is all over, I'll explain everything if Chad is still willing to listen.*

She grabbed her purse and headed downstairs.

Chapter 23

"I'M here to collect the books."

Heather pressed her lips together, suppressing a grin, as she glanced from Ashley to Chad. Gazing into Chad's eyes was more than she could handle at the moment, so she looked up at Makki, staring down at her from on top of the book shelf.

Chad headed toward the back room. "The books are in two fabric tote bags in the back. I'll load them in your car for you."

"I can load them myself." She followed him.

He handed her the totes. "Is something wrong?"

"No." She chuckled. "I'm good."

She grabbed the totes and took a deep breath to calm down. "I'm sure the residents of the retirement village will appreciate these." Then she headed out the back door and slipped into her car.

She'd have to tell Chad everything soon, or this whole thing could blow up in her face. A serious talk with Aunt Julia was in the iminent future, too. Whether her aunt realized it or not, they needed more help than Christine Talan could give them.

Heather's stomach growled, reminding her she hadn't eaten lunch, and it was nearly two. She stopped at the *Club Car Diner* for a hot dog and a Pepsi.

***

At the retirement village, Heather checked in with the director and handed the books over to her.

"Can you tell me where the lady who's doing community service is right now?"

"Yes, I believe Julia's still helping out in the kitchen. Or she may be in one of the rooms on the main floor, reading to, or playing games with, some of our residents."

"Thanks."

The kitchen was locked, so Heather wandered through the hallway until she came to a comfortably paneled open room with a white marble fireplace, several over-stuffed recliners, and a few random tables. Her aunt was seated at a table, in serious conversation with three elderly residents, as she wrote on a sheet of ledger paper.

Heather scurried over to her. "How's your day going?"

Julia jumped and turned to face her niece, slapping her hand on top of the paper. "What are you doing here?"

I came to check up on you. "I have something to tell you."

"Couldn't it wait until I got home?"

"I'm afraid not."

Julia glanced around the table. "Where are my manners? Let me introduce you to my new friends. Heather Stanton's my niece. This is Eloise Brown, Hank Hutchinson, and his brother Leonard."

Heather shook hands with each one. "Delighted to meet you all."

Hank elbowed Leonard. "She's a pretty one, with red hair like her aunt, ain't she?"

Leonard nodded with a noticeably false-toothy smile. "Yeah, yeah, nice ta meetcha." Eloise tapped her index finger on the table. "Now can we get back to what we were doing?"

Julia grabbed the paper along with a pamphlet and shoved them into her large, chartreuse purse, but not before Heather caught a glimpse of the name at the top of the pamphlet. *Daily Racing Form.*

Wasn't this just like her aunt? "You're collecting money from these people to bet on horses?"

"Naw," Leonard said. "They don't allow gambling here."

"It's only for the Kentucky Derby tomorrow," Eloise added. "Julia's acting as our bookie."

"But Aunt Julia, you can't..."

Julia scrunched her eyes and put a finger to her lips. "It's only a bit of fun. Everyone bets on the Derby."

"Julia's given us a winning horse too," Eloise said. "His name is Fatal."

Heather saw the connection with what had happened to Esther and the name of the horse. In Julia's own lingo, she asked, "So, what are the odds on, Fatal?"

"Twenty-to-one." Leonard shoved a twenty dollar bill at Julia. "Here, take my money, and put it on Fatal's nose."

Julia grabbed the bill. "I'll give you a little betting advice. The best way to bet on a horse is for it to *show*. If it finishes in one of the top three slots: *win, place,* or *show*, you win. They also call this, 'betting across the board,' but it would cost you three times as much to bet money on each."

Hank waved his bills in the air. "Here's my money. I'll bet twenty bucks across the board."

"Please," Julia said. "A little decorum, if you don't mind." She glanced from side to side, grabbed the money, and shoved it in her purse.

Heather smiled at the three residents. "Since your *bookie* business is over, I have to talk to my aunt. Will you excuse us for a moment?" She pulled Julia to the side and brought her voice down to a whisper. "When I tried to find the other shoe back at the apartment this morning, it was gone."

"What do you mean, *gone?*"

"I can't find it anywhere. When I arrived home from the field, Makki was in the apartment, and the newspaper the shoe had been wrapped in was shredded. The cat may have done something with it."

Julia stood silent for a moment as if she was thinking over this latest development. "Well, then it's out of our hands." A moment later, her eyelashes nearly touched her brows. "Uh oh, I think the poop is about to hit the fan."

Heather turned. Detective Lindsey headed in their direction with a defiance to his steps.

Julia bee-lined it out the door as she slipped a peppermint into her mouth. Heather started after her aunt, but the Detective detoured down a hallway and got to Julia first. Heather could only stand behind them and watch.

"Hello, Ms. Fairchild. We need to talk."

"About what?"

"The warehouse fire. I'm questioning all persons of interest."

"Why am I *of interest?*"

"I have my reasons. Come down to the station with me."

"Now?" Julia checked her watch. "I still have two hours of community service time to finish before I can leave."

"I'll expect you there when your time is over for the day." Detective Lindsey handed Julia his card. "If there's a problem, call me, anytime."

As he walked out, Julia flapped a hand after him. "Yeah, and that's not all I'll call you." She popped another mint into her mouth.

"Don't be so hard on him. He's only doing his job."

"I refuse to listen to anything more about the man." Julia raised a finger. "However, before we were interrupted, I was listening to some juicy gossip, right from the horses' mouths, so to speak."

Julia led Heather back to the table. "Eloise, Hank, and Leonard all knew Esther Kwinn."

"Were you friends with her?" Heather asked the trio.

"Sort of," Eloise said. "Over the years, on and off. But she had an acid tongue."

"Yeah, when she got old." Leonard affirmed. "She wasn't always like that. I remember as a young woman, she was beautiful, and fun. Two unfortunate marriages can sometimes make a person bitter. Lately, I could tell something was wrong. She acted nervous and jumpy."

"All I know is," Eloise said, "her ex was back in town, and that annoyed her. She never loved him, or Doctor Kwinn, rest his soul. Not like she did Mr. Willows. After he passed away, she went into some kind of depression. He was her first love. She waited so many years to be with him, and after only a few months, he was gone. It broke the poor woman's heart… again."

"He broke her heart before?" Julia asked.

"When they were young. Willows's father didn't approve."

"She wasn't rich enough," Hank said. "He did everything he could to keep them apart. Pressured his son into marrying his business partner's daughter. I'm not saying they weren't happy, because it appeared they were. I'm only saying Esther was devastated. She married Bax on the rebound."

"Sometimes it's the way things work out." Julia sighed. "We can't always have who we want." She stared into the distance as if recalling an unrequited love of her own.

"Could she have been meeting Bax the morning she was killed?" Heather asked.

"I doubt it," Eloise said. "She was signed up for the seniors' water aerobics class at the park field house. He's not a member."

Leonard leaned in closer. "Or maybe she was meeting Madam Z for some kind of sunrise satanic ritual."

Hank nudged Leonard. "Personally, I think Esther was in a Voodoo trance when she got there, or she was put into one soon after she arrived."

"Sounds about right," Leonard continued. "Madam Z is always doing rituals or performing them on people. And she has this magic elixir—."

Hank cleared his throat, like they were in a conspiracy of secrecy.

Leonard glanced at his brother and stuttered. "I mean, everyone knows the madam worships Satan in the wooded area behind her studio, at midnight, during a full moon. She made a huge clearing for herself and placed an enormous Baphomet Goat gargoyle statue in it. I looked it up. It's supposed to be a guard. Gives me the heebie-jeebies. The word around town is if you touch it, you'll have bad luck for the rest of your life."

"We saw one of her rituals on a full moon night, about seven years ago," Hank said. "Didn't we, Eloise?"

"Yeah. She chopped the head off a live chicken, then she poured the blood into a silver goblet and put it to her lips. We didn't stick around to watch anymore, and we never went back."

"Ugh! Sounds Gruesome." Heather shivered. *But I saw all of you come out the back door of her studio when I had dinner at the Vendeglo.*

Julia crinkled her nose. "She may not do bizarre stuff like that anymore."

Leonard leaned in closer. "We hear she does worse. The scuttlebutt around town is she was trying to contact Satan to bring Willows back from the dead."

Eloise puffed. "I don't care what anybody says, you can't bring dead people back." She glanced at Heather with hooded, gray eyes. "Can you?"

Does she need reassurance? "Of course not. It's silly to believe anyone can."

Julia leaned her elbows on the table and rubbed her hands together, like she'd come up with a better idea. "Maybe she was only trying to contact his spirit."

Eloise leaned back in her chair and crossed her arms. "I wouldn't be surprised."

Heather rubbed the mild ache in her temples. *These people are hard to fathom.* "Are there any *real* people who might have had a motive to kill Esther?"

Hank stared down at his hands. "No one specific. We heard her arguing with her ex, and we even heard her arguing with your aunt once."

"I'm not sure how long she was going to be around," Eloise said. "Living here ain't cheap, you know. And she was a gambler."

Aunt Julia told me it costs over four thousand dollars a month.

"If you ask me," Eloise continued, "She was running out of money. Maybe she asked Madam Z for a loan."

Heather glanced at her aunt. "You should mention Esther's money problems to Detective Lindsey when you see him later."

Julia's eyes scrunched. "He probably already knows."

"Yeah, we told the police." Hank flapped his hand. "But they don't listen to anything we have to say."

I can understand why. Especially if you told them about Madam Z trying to bring Mr. Willows back from the dead.

"Well," Julia said. "It's been a delight talking to you, but I have another assignment. I'll place your bets on the Derby tomorrow." She waved a hand at them as she led Heather out the door.

"What other assignment do you have?"

Julia opened her purse and pulled out a key. "We have to check out Esther's apartment."

"How did you get that?"

"Tell you later. Come in with me. Please."

They took the elevator to the second floor and got off. Checking the door numbers, they found the one matching the key tag. Standing in front of it, Heather couldn't bring herself to move. "Is this ethical?"

"Ethics, smethics. What does that mean, anyway? We're not breaking and entering. I have the key." Julia turned it in the lock and opened the door.

Light gray living room curtains hung across the tall windows allowing bright sunlight to warm the rectangular room. Heather followed her aunt into the living area filled with cream-colored, French Provencal furniture and dozens of candles in every size, shape, and color. "She must have been expecting a power outage."

"No." Julia stood in the middle of the room and turned in a circle. "She was expecting something evil."

"Then she wasted a lot of money on candles." Heather walked over to a small desk in the corner near the window. "The police have already been here and searched, so we may not find anything useful."

Julia headed to the bedroom.

Opening the top drawer of the desk, Heather rummaged through a short stack of papers. "I don't see anything here but a few bills and ads. Nothing to connect anyone to Esther's murder."

Heather opened the side drawer and pulled out a black pen, a silver letter opener, and a few paper clips. She fingered the inside of the drawer to see if anything was left in the back. *A notch?* She stuck her middle finger in it and flipped up the wood to reveal a sheet of parchment underneath.

"Aunt Julia."

"What is it?" Julia called from the bedroom.

Heather pulled out the paper and studied it. "It looks like an old government grant to some land." She grabbed her cell phone and took pictures as Julia came out to join her.

"Let me see." Julia scanned the page. She folded the paper and put it in her purse."

"Put it back."

Julia leaned into her. "But it might be useful."

"I snapped photos of it."

Ringggg!

Heather jumped.

"It's just the telephone." Julia snickered. "Not many people have land lines these days."

Heart racing, Heather was tempted to answer it. "I wonder who could be calling?"

No name came up on the caller ID, just a number. She wrote the number down and waited for the voice mail to pick up, but the caller hung up.

Julia strolled over to the phone. "There might be something useful on the voicemail."

Heather pressed the message button: "You have two old messages. Wednesday, May 25th, 1:00 p.m. *'Hello Mrs. Quinn. It's Jennifer from Willows Bend Realty. Mr. Brown can see you tomorrow afternoon at two p.m. in his office. If you can't make it, please call back. You have our number.'*"

"The appointment's for the day she was killed," Heather said. "We'll have to find out why she was seeing a real estate agent. Maybe it has something to do with the land grant."

"I'm writing his name down," Julia said.

The second message came up: "Wednesday, May 24th, 4:00 p.m. *'I have cleared time for you. Come to me at seven o'clock.'*"

Heather recognized the mysterious sounding voice as Madam Z's. She glanced at her aunt. "It's your friend. But did she want Esther to be there at seven the same evening, or seven on the morning she was killed?"

"If it was in the morning, maybe they were doing a sunrise ritual, like Leonard said, and something went horribly wrong." Julia let out a breath of relief. "It could have been an accident."

"If it was, why didn't the madam report it to the police?"

"Let them figure it out." Julia turned and headed toward the bathroom. "I'm checking in here."

Heather came in as Julia opened the medicine cabinet. Besides toothpaste and brushes, heartburn tablets, a prescription for blood thinner, and one for high blood pressure, there was a small, black bottle.

Madam Z's Magic Elixir. She turned it over. "A mixture of herbs and flowers. It's good for what is bad."

"What do you suppose Esther was taking this elixir for?"

"Whatever was bad in her life. The madam makes it up special for each of her clients."

"And charges a fortune for it."

"She doesn't sell her elixirs," Julia said. "She gives them away to those who require her help."

There could be shoe polish in it for all anyone knows. Heather unscrewed the top and sniffed. A strong, medicinal odor irritated her eyes. She shuddered, blinked the tears away, and put the top back on.

Then she picked up a box of over-the-counter sleeping pills. "Looks like she took these too."

"They help a lot. I take them occasionally."

Could explain the sleepwalking.

A click at the front door alerted Heather. She froze. "Someone's coming in," she whispered to her aunt and stepped into the bathtub. Julia closed the cabinet door, and followed her in. She pulled the shower curtain around them.

Heather held her breath. *I hope it's not the police.*

Not long after the front door closed, thrashing sounds from the living room signaled that someone was searching the place. *I hope whoever it is doesn't decide to come in here. But just in case...*

She shoved her hand into her purse, grabbed her pepper spray container, and fingered the trigger.

Chapter 24

THE noises escalated by the minute and got nearer to the bathroom. A man's voice mumbled as drawers opened and slammed shut. With every sound, Heather's shoulders twitched. Then heavy footsteps headed in their direction.

Heather poised the pepper spray at face level. But the intruder didn't come in. *He must have gone into the bedroom.* She breathed a sigh of relief and stepped out of the tub to peek through the open door. The short, gray-haired man wearing the brown bomber jacket, was busy in a frantic search through the items on the bedroom closet shelf.

She put a finger to her lips and motioned her aunt to leave the bathroom. They tiptoed to the front door. A familiar smoky scent lingered in the air and caught in her throat.

Julia turned the knob and opened the door enough for her and Heather to squeeze through. Then she pressed it closed. From the sounds the man made as he threw things around, Heather was sure he hadn't heard them.

"Let's get out of here," Julia said. "But first, I have to put the key back from where I pinched it. And then I have to check in with the administrator."

Delighted her aunt was doing the right thing, Heather said, "I'll meet you out front in ten minutes." *How much trouble can she get into in ten minutes?*

Julia scurried toward the steps.

Heather's cell rang. Chad's ID came up.

"Hi," she said as she made her way to the elevator.

"A heads-up. Detective Lindsey is heading to the retirement village to bring your aunt in for questioning about the fire."

"Thanks. But he was already here. My aunt still had some time to serve today, so I'm driving her to the station now."

"I wanted you to know the investigation showed the cause of the fire was arson. A witness saw your aunt at the scene minutes before it started, so guess who their number one *person of interest* is?"

***

At the station, Detective Lindsey took the chair across from Julia and loosened his tie, like he was expecting this to be a long session.

"Do you mind if I sit in?" Heather asked. "I'd like to support my aunt."

His thick fingers drummed the wood as Julia stared at the red stiletto sandal in the plastic evidence bag on the desk in front of her. "I don't mind. You might be of help."

His gaze then landed on Julia's face. "Do you recognize this shoe?"

"Of course I do. It's a woman's shoe, size eight and a half, and it's covered in, what looks like, mud."

"It's ash. What can you tell me about it?"

Julia scrunched her face. "Ummm… nothing."

He glanced at Heather. "How about you?"

Heather pressed her lips together. As long as her aunt wasn't talking, neither was she.

The Detective placed both hands on the desk and leaned forward. "Well, one of you had better come up with *something*."

Julia calmed her demeanor. "All I can say is, the shoe doesn't belong to me. Period." She stood. "Are we done?"

Lindsey smirked. "We're far from done." He pointed to the chair. "Sit!"

Julia lowered herself into it and raised an eyebrow.

"We know the shoe belongs to Kystal Stamos." He leaned back in his chair. "We've already talked to her. She told us you came to her house yesterday to accuse her dad of theft."

Julia nodded. "He stole a race ticket from me. It's worth thousands, and I was hoping she'd be gracious enough to hand it over. But she wouldn't even let me look for it."

"She told me you tripped her and then stole her shoes."

Julia popped a tiny mint into her mouth and raised a finger. "*Allegedly* tripped her, and I don't steal things."

No, you borrow them.

"Then can you tell me why you were seen wearing the shoes later the same night, in the field near the paper recycling center before the building went up in flames?"

Beads of sweat broke on Julia's upper lip. Either she was feeling the heat from Lindsey, or her nerves were unraveling. Heather hoped she'd break soon. All this covering up was more than she could handle.

Julia sucked in a long, slow breath and let it out. "So I was there."

"You admit you were in the field wearing those shoes?"

Julia clicked her tongue. "That's what I said, isn't it?"

Lindsey snickered, like he'd finally made a dent in Julia's armor. "What were you doing there?"

Julia folded her arms. "I was trying to find a certain spot."

"You mean the best place to start the building on fire?"

Julia's eyes widened. "Now you're putting words in my mouth."

Lindsey wagged a finger at her. "Don't bother to deny it. We have a witness who saw you light up a huge bundle of paper near the building."

How will she talk her way out of this?

"A witness, huh?" Julia's shoulders dropped. "I didn't see anyone."

Heather rubbed her thumbnail across her bottom lip and nearly bit the nail off. She couldn't hold the words in any longer.

"For goodness sake, you might as well tell him everything. The police have a way of finding these things out."

Julia tsked. "All right. I'll come clean."

Finally!

"But keep a couple of things in mind, Detective. I had no intention of setting the building on fire, nor did I have a motive.

Elbows on the desk, he tented his fingers. "I'm listening."

***

All through Julia's explanation of what had happened the day of the fire, Lindsey leaned forward in his chair, lips curved into a frown.

As Julia finished her story, Lindsey burst into laughter. "A ritual to get rid of a curse? That's the most ridiculous thing I've ever heard." He could barely get the words out.

"If you're finished ridiculing me, can I leave?"

He stood, with a grin still on his lips, and walked to the door. "Yeah, you're free to go—for now."

Julia's jaw dropped. "You mean it's over? But aren't you going to...?" She lifted an eyebrow. "Wait a minute. You have information you're not telling me, don't you?"

Heather grabbed her aunt's arm. *She's not digging herself in any deeper.* "Don't push it. If the detective sees no reason to detain us, then let's go."

Lindsey lifted a finger. "There's one more thing. We'll be looking for the other shoe. And if we find it in your apartment, Krystal will press charges for theft."

Julia huffed. "I swear to you, I don't have it."

Coaxing her aunt out the door wasn't easy. Heather wanted to tell the detective what they'd seen in Esther's apartment and heard from the people at the retirement village, but they had no business being there or questioning people. She'd have to find another way to inform the police, without getting either one of them involved.

Julia got into Heather's rental car and buckled herself in. "Lindsey's interview left me with an uneasy feeling, like there's something troublesome hanging over my head, ready to drop at the most inopportune moment." She glanced at her cell phone. "I know what will make me feel better—a delicious bowl of goulash. Let's have dinner at the Vendeglo restaurant."

"We eat out so much. It's getting expensive."

Julia shook her head as if she felt sorry for Heather. "Don't you know how to get out of paying a restaurant tab?"

Heather gripped the steering wheel tighter. "No. And I don't want to know."

"It's about time you learned. Leave everything to me. When we get there, order us both something from the bar. It's Friday night, and we'll probably have to wait for a table anyway. Meanwhile, I'll have a quick chat with Mad... um, and be back in a Chicago Second."

"You mean, a New York Minute?"

"Same thing."

Heather was fortunate to find a place to park in the crowded restaurant lot. Julia opened the passenger door as Heather turned off the engine.

Before she got out, Heather asked, "Why do you need to talk to Madam Z now?"

"My curse-ridding ritual went up in flames last night. I have to find out how to fix it."

"Doesn't it seem like Madam Z set you up to take the blame for this arson?"

"How would she know I'd ruin the ritual?"

"Maybe she set you up to fail."

"Now you're talking crazy." Julia tossed her wild hair back. "Why would she do that?"

So she wouldn't be blamed for it?

As Julia headed to the madam's studio, Heather made her way to the restaurant. She opened the stained-glass door, but the entrance was blocked by couples waiting for tables. Her aunt was right. There would be a wait.

Heather excused her way to the front of the line. Her heart sank. Why couldn't Miklos be manning the reservation desk tonight?

Sandy glanced up at her, and a quick grin lit up his tanned face. "Well, hello there, Beautiful." His tone was warm, welcoming, and extremely annoying—like the shrill sound of a whistle on a tea kettle. "Do you have a reservation?"

She forced a smile. "No, I'm afraid I don't. I—"

"We don't have tables for one, but if you'll wait a few minutes until my brother relieves me, I'll join you for dinner."

No thank you. "As I was saying before you interrupted me, I'm meeting my aunt here. But we'll be glad to wait for a table. How long will it be?"

Sandy's smile slipped. "About a half hour. But for you, I'll see what I can do to hurry things up. If you'll wait at the bar, I'll have the bartender make you my special drink."

I hate when men assume they know what I like without asking. "It's kind of you to offer, but I'm the designated driver tonight, so I won't be drinking."

At the bar, she ordered herself seltzer water with a twist of lime and a brandy for her aunt.

No sooner had the bartender put the drinks on the counter, than Julia came running in with a wide-eyed grimace on her face. She grabbed the brandy from the counter and gulped it down.

Heather was almost afraid to ask.

"What's wrong?"

Chapter 25

JULIA glanced around the restaurant, as if she was searching for someone. "She's not here. She's not in her store either."

"Then you can see her later or tomorrow morning."

Julia set her empty glass on the bar. "No. You don't understand. She's not anywhere. Her place is dark and closed up, like she was never there. She's not answering her door bell, my phone calls, or my texts. It's not like her. She's always available."

"Not if she's with another client. Everyone's not available all the time. Maybe she's taking a bath or she's asleep. She could have gone out of town on an emergency. Relax, you can always see her tomorrow."

"She said she'd be here for me, no matter what."

"There are always circumstances. And people do lie."

Julia rubbed her forehead. "True. But I can't believe ..." She tapped her short red nails on the bar to catch the bartender's attention. "Another brandy, please."

"Having another drink won't help."

"It'll make me feel better."

Heather lowered her voice. "About her being a charlatan?"

"I didn't say that. Something must have happened to her. Maybe she's been kidnapped. Or worse."

"Now who's talking crazy?"

"I didn't think anyone spoke that language." Sandy's deep, baritone blundered into the middle of their conversation.

Heather turned her head. "Hi."

His round, grinning face beamed at her. "Glad you're still at the bar here. Good news. I have a table for us."

Julia fixated on him with wide-eyed enthusiasm. "Thanks." She grabbed Sandy's muscular, snake-tattooed arm. "I'm starving. Does this mean you'll be joining us? Lead the way."

Heather sucked in a breath, pressed her lips together, and glared at her aunt with a *I don't want to have dinner with this guy* look—which Julia ignored.

Why do I bother?

Sandy led them to a table near the front door.

"But this is a table for two," Julia said.

"That's easily remedied." He pulled a chair from a nearby table being vacated and slid it under theirs. Then he motioned to a waiter. "Menus over here, please."

All Heather could do was smile. Now she was stuck, but at least she wasn't alone with him. As he lowered himself into the seat across from her, Julia gave Heather one of those smiles that told her Sandy was going to be useful. And she didn't wait to start in on him.

"I went to visit Madam Z, but she wasn't there. The place is locked up. Any idea where she went or how long she'll be gone?"

"I didn't realize she was gone. No one keeps an eye on her. She pretty much comes and goes as she pleases. But I have to admit, I haven't seen her today. Maybe she's at one of those Pagan Ritual Festivals she attends."

"How long do they usually last?"

"Sometimes one night and other times a week or two, in which case I pick up her mail when I see it piling up."

Julia jumped out of her chair, eyes wide, hands in her hair. "A couple of weeks? I can't wait that long to see her."

Heather stood and placed a hand on her aunt's tense shoulder, as other diners turned their attention to her.

"Relax. There isn't anything you can do about it. Sit down, and we'll order dinner."

Julia chugged the rest of her drink. It apparently worked like a tranquilizer. She sat silent for a few moments, and then she blinked several times as if she'd come to her senses. "You're right. I'll deal with this problem later."

This wasn't a positive statement. Whenever Julia instantly calmed down after a blowup, she'd usually thought of an idea that would get them both into trouble.

***

The waiter brought coffee to their table after a tasty meal. Julia motioned toward the front door with her head. She stood and patted Sandos on the shoulder. "Thanks for dinner. It was delicious, but my niece and I have a million things to do tonight. Tomorrow's Derby Day."

Sandos stood. "I know. It's one of our busiest days. But surely you can stay for dessert."

Heather picked up on Julia's cue. "My aunt's right. It was a delicious dinner. My compliments to your chef. Now I need the check."

"No check." Sandos grinned. "Dinner's on me."

"Thanks. It was kind of you. Goodnight." Heather said the words as quickly as she could and followed Julia out. She was never so glad to leave a restaurant.

Sandos stuck his head around the door and yelled, "I'll call you."

She wanted to turn around and say, "Don't bother," but it would be rude, and she was taught never be uncouth, so she waved a half-hearted acknowledgement.

Julia rushed to the parking lot and headed for the car but stopped a few feet shy of it.

Heather strolled up behind her. "What things do you have to do?"

"I don't have time to lollygag around here while a tattooed bodybuilder makes goo-goo eyes at you when I can be doing something more important."

Heather was relieved her aunt made the excuse to leave the restaurant, but she couldn't imagine what her "more important things" could be. "Like what?"

Julia headed toward the other side of the parking lot. Heather caught up with her. "Where are you going?"

"I have to make sure Madam Z's safe. I'm telling you, something's wrong. She wouldn't disappear like a thief in the night. Not voluntarily."

"Why not tell the police, and let them handle it?"

"She hasn't been missing long enough. If I don't hear from her in the morning, then I might, but right now I have to investigate."

"I'll go with you, but only to make sure nothing's suspicious."

Julia wiggled the knob on Madam Z's back door and knocked on the window as Heather inspected the grounds behind the building adjacent to the sprawling wooded area.

There was nothing to suspect anything sinister had happened there.

A short walk deeper into the woods showed an immense clearing where the ground had been kicked up and trampled as if some event had taken place recently. Then she turned and bumped into the huge, gray, stone goat gargoyle that towered over her, complete with wings, horns, and hideous teeth. Heather shuddered and hurried back to where Julia stooped at the back door, holding a thin rod in her hand as if she was trying to force the lock.

"Stop it!"

Julia jumped to her feet and shoved the rod into her purse. "What? I... um, was checking if a key was in the lock on the other side of the door."

"Nothing appears suspicious out here, except for the giant gargoyle statue in the woods."

"You didn't touch it, did you?"

I may have bumped it by accident. "Even if I did, it's nothing more than a large piece of gruesome-looking carved stone. It doesn't have any powers."

Julia gave her a side glance. "You don't know that for sure."

Yes, I do.

On the way back to Heather's rental car, Julia shuffled her feet. "Nothing may seem suspicious from the outside, but there might be something sinister going on inside. We'll have to come back later to check it out, when it's dark."

"There's no way I'm coming back here later." Heather started the engine and gave her aunt a narrow-eyed glare. It was the best she could do. There was nothing she could say to stop her.

Chapter 26

H EATHER drove her car into town where rows of cars lined the streets and crowds of people mobbed the sidewalks. "What's going on here?"

"Must be because it's Kentucky Derby weekend, along with the grand re-opening of the off-track betting parlor."

I forgot.

Heather drove to her parking spot behind the bookstore. It was taken, and Chad was parked in his usual spot. She drove through the ally and rounded the corner. Every available parking spot was filled. Then she drove down block after block only to find no parking spaces.

Julia craned her neck to gaze out the window. "Park in the hotel lot. We can walk back. It's not far."

"And get towed? No thank you. Somebody has to pull out of a parking space eventually."

"We can't drive around all night waiting. I'll call Christine." Julia pulled out her phone. "We can park in her driveway while I fill her in on what's been happening, and then she can drive us back. She tapped in Christine's number.

"Hi Chris, it's Julia. Have I got news! Do you mind if Heather and I come over?" A short pause. "Oh. I see. Well sure, I understand."

Julia put the phone in her purse and folded her arms. "Huh!"

"What's wrong?"

"George came home early." After a few minutes, Julia pointed out the front windshield. "The movie theater's only a couple blocks away. We can park in their lot."

"They tow cars too."

"Not if we see the movie."

It had been a long day, and Heather wouldn't be able to keep her eyes open through an entire movie. Besides it would be another unnecessary expense. But at this moment, it seemed like their only option. "You win."

***

Two hours later, they walked out of the theater into the cool, refreshing night air. Heather stretched. The movie had held her attention through the first half but failed to keep her awake for the second.

The crowd in the parking lot was worse than the one on the sidewalk earlier, but they finally made their way to the car. Heather drove to the bookstore and turned into the alley. One parking spot was open. Chad's spot. *He must have just gone home.*

Heather parked and followed her aunt up the back stairs.

Inside their apartment, she switched on the kitchen light and brewed a cup of chamomile tea, grabbing a donut from a plate on the counter. She didn't have dessert after dinner, and now she was hungry.

"I'm glad I don't have to work tomorrow." Julia leaned against the counter for support while she flipped off her shoes. She headed toward the living room, and turned on the table lamp. "Did you ever get the remote fixed?"

Heather slipped out of her shoes and followed her aunt. "Yes, Chad found the real remote earlier today. I put it next to the flat screen."

Julia switched on the TV. The local news station came up with information about the warehouse fire. During the investigation, a body had been found among the rubble. It hadn't been identified yet, but they were working on it. The weather was up next.

Heather's throat tightened. She set the donut on the end table and eased herself onto the sofa. "This is awful."

"You're telling me." Julia plopped down next to her. "Another dead body! Who'll be next? When will it end? The curse is getting worse, and I can't locate Madam Z." She jumped up and paced the floor.

"I doubt if this latest death has anything to do with your curse, so please calm down. Let's think about this rationally." Heather grabbed the donut and took a bite. Then she picked up her teacup. "Maybe Esther's murder, Madam Z's disappearance, the fire, and the dead person, are somehow all connected."

"Yeah, they're all connected to the curse."

Heather tried to ignore her aunt's remark, but she couldn't. "You can't blame every unfortunate thing that happens on the curse."

She waited for a defensive answer, but Julia gave none, so she finished the donut and drank the last of her tea. Before she left the kitchen, Heather filled a glass with water to set on her nightstand. "Have you found anything good on TV?

Julia yawned. "Nothing new. Think I'll stay up and watch reruns for a while."

***

Heather was startled awake by a ring tone. She rolled over in bed and grabbed her cell from the night stand. *Who's calling me at one in the morning? This had better be important.*

"Hello?" She answered in a gruff voice.

"Hi, it's your aunt. Now, don't fly off the handle when I tell you where I am."

Heather sat up. "I thought you were in bed."

"I got restless watching TV, and I started worrying about Madam Z. She might've been locked up in her studio, unconscious. I called Christine. She wasn't asleep either, so she snuck out of the house while George was sleeping, and we drove over to check out the place."

"Let me guess. You got arrested for breaking and entering, and you're at the police station. Am I right?"

"Well, sort of."

"Did you get arrested, or didn't you?"

"We were lucky. Officer Henderson came by in his patrol car. I explained what we were doing there and what I suspected, and asked him to check out the place."

"More like, you insisted."

"No matter. Please pick me up. I'll tell you all about it when you get here."

Heather swung her legs over the side of the bed. "Give me fifteen minutes. And please don't say or do anything to antagonize anyone."

Sixteen minutes later, Heather blinked her sleepy eyes against the fluorescent lights as she trudged into the police station.

She addressed the patrolman at the front desk. "Hi. Where is she?"

He jerked his thumb at a vacant desk behind him.

Heather nodded her appreciation.

Julia dropped her cell phone into her purse and stood as Heather approached her. "Thanks for coming to get me. What would I do without you?"

Heather was beginning to wonder herself. "Please, get in the car."

She addressed the officer. "Any charges?"

"No. Henderson gave Ms. Fairchild a caution."

"Thank him for me."

The officer smiled. "Will do."

In the car, Heather sat in the driver's seat and folded her arms. "What happened?"

"I explained to Henderson what I suspected, and he checked the outside with his flashlight. But he said he didn't see anything suspicious. And then I told him I smelled gas. Christine backed me up. So he broke the back window and told us to wait outside. As if we'd stay put. We tiptoed in behind him."

"Was she there?"

"We didn't see her. But while he investigated the kitchen, I searched the back room and noticed a computer, a monitor, and a printer. Christine opened a few of the desk drawers before Henderson came back. We found files on a lot of people."

"It must be how she knows so much. She's probably been keeping information on the residents in this town for years."

Julia took a paper out of her pocket. "I managed to snatch this off the printer before Henderson forced us out of the house."

Heather turned on the car engine. "What is it?"

"A train schedule. Could she have left town?"

"It would explain why she's not around."

"I noticed Madam Z didn't take the book of spells with her. She wouldn't leave it behind, so she must still be here."

"What book of spells?"

"The one with the gold-tipped pages. It could hold all of her accumulated knowledge about the occult. Since the back door window is broken anyway, I can slip inside and grab it, quick like."

"Not tonight. The only place you're going is back to our apartment. You can check out the book on the internet to see what's in it. By the way, what happened to Christine?"

"Officer Henderson let her go home. Then he brought me to the station and told me to call you. I guess he didn't want me spending the night there again."

Heather could understand why. The last time her aunt was in the lockup, she gave the police one heck of a hard time.

***

At the apartment, Heather glanced over the paper Julia had taken from Madam Z's printer.

"This train schedule has today's date on it."

Julia filled a glass with water from the refrigerator. "If she left town, she could be miles away by now. And the curse is still on my head." She took a gulp of water and headed for Heather's laptop. "I'll browse the Internet for the book and see what it holds."

Heather waited for her aunt to do a search.

A few moments later, Julia's eyes glistened. "I found it. '*The Garden of Shadows* explains the secret knowledge of trees and herbs as delivered by the Fallen Angels unto mankind.' I told you it held secrets, and probably spells and incantations too."

Heather yawned. "But you don't know what secrets. They might not have anything to do with curses. Now that you have your answer, I'm going to bed, and I suggest you do the same."

But Heather's suggestions were hardly ever heeded by her aunt.

Chapter 27

"WAKE up, Sleepy Head. It's Kentucky Derby Day." Julia's voice drifted into Heather's ears in the guise of a dream. Was she actually being spoken to? She opened her eyes and checked her cell phone for the time. "Seven-thirty?"

Julia walked into her room with a cup in one hand and a paper in the other. "It's Derby Day, and the first race starts at ten-thirty. We want to be at the off-track betting parlor when the place opens at eight."

"This morning?"

"Yes. It opens at the same time as Churchill Downs."

"I thought the Kentucky Derby ran later today."

"It does, but there are also thirteen other races. The actual Derby will be run at approximately six-fifty this evening. But I want to be there for all the races. I'll be placing gradual bets on most of them before the Derby. Hurry up and get dressed. We don't want to miss watching the Garland of Roses arrive at the clubhouse gate around nine forty-five."

Heather put her head back on the pillow and closed her eyes. "Sorry, but I'm tired from being awakened out of a sound sleep at one in the morning to pick you up at the police station."

"What are you complaining about? You don't have to go to the office today or any day. You may not have to work ever again if you bet enough on the right horse to win the Derby."

"And I suppose the winning horse's name is *Fatal*."

"I have an idea, but remember what I told the folks at the retirement village about betting to win, place, or show. My sources are not infallible." Julia waved her cup in the air. "Get dressed, and I'll make pancakes for breakfast. Or better yet, we can eat breakfast there."

Heather didn't want to have breakfast at the off-track betting parlor, no matter how fashionably it had been renovated. Spending time with Krystal Stamos was the last thing she wanted to do today or ever again.

"No thanks. I'll stay here and make my own breakfast."

"Why don't you want to come with me?"

"I'm not interested in betting on horses all day. Besides, I doubt if Krystal will be overjoyed to see us after our visit to her house the other evening. Especially since she's convinced you stole her shoes."

"She has no proof. Besides, thanks to Makki, I don't have the other shoe." Julia lifted Heather's shoulder bag from the counter and handed it to her. "At least drive me."

"You'll have to walk. I'm not moving my car from its parking space, or I may never find another one with the crowds in town this weekend."

Julia slipped into her walking shoes. "All right. I'll walk." She grabbed her large chartreuse purse. "Meet me there for The Derby race. Betting starts around six-thirty."

"That one, I wouldn't miss. And good luck with the other races."

Julia checked over the racing form and tsked. "I don't need luck. I've got knowhow."

***

Pancakes sounded great for breakfast. Heather dressed and whipped up a batch from a mix. Whatever she didn't eat, she'd freeze for later in the week.

She got comfortable at the kitchen counter and picked up the maple syrup as a key turned in the front door. Julia sauntered in, flung her purse down on the cocktail table, and plopped on the sofa.

Heather slid off the kitchen stool. "Why are you back so soon?"

"I hate Krystal Stamos." Julia drummed her short fingernails on the end table. "She banned me from the off-track betting parlor. The bouncer at the door wouldn't let me in."

Not unexpected.

Julia raised a fist. "She can't do that."

"It's her establishment. She can ban whomever she wants."

"Be that as it may, I still gave the guy a piece of my mind." She wiped tears away with her fingers. "I've waited all year for this, and now I have to miss it."

I knew something like this would happen. But Heather didn't want to argue with her aunt. Not when she was feeling so low. "You can still bet on the races, can't you?"

Julia gave out a long, slow sigh as her body went limp. "Sure, I can place bets with my bookie. But it's not only the betting. It's the camaraderie, the spirit of the day, the decorations, the excitement of watching the races."

"Since you have to stay home, have some pancakes. I made a fresh batch."

I think I saw a television in the backroom of the store downstairs. They might have cable. Heather checked her watch. "Maybe there's something I can do." She pressed Chad's number on her cell.

He picked up on the first ring. "Hi Heather."

Her stomach fluttered as it always did when she heard his voice. "I've made pancakes for breakfast and was wondering if you and your sister would like to have some before you open the bookstore this morning."

"Thanks for the invitation, but we're not opening the bookstore today. Our grandfather learned, from years of experience, it was a waste of time to open on Derby Day."

"Oh, I'm sorry to hear that."

"Why?"

"I was hoping my aunt could watch the races on the TV in the back room, if you have cable."

"We do, but why doesn't she go to the off-track betting parlor?" He sucked in a breath, as if he'd recalled something. "Oh, yeah. She's probably been banned."

"You guessed it."

"Well, I can understand why. I mean, with the shoe situation and the other charge. Why don't you and your aunt come to our house. You can watch the races here. We've got Churchill Downs streaming right now."

I can't think of a better way to spend the day. "Fantastic. I'll bring the pancakes and syrup, and we can eat breakfast at your place."

"I'll tell Ashley to make sausages. See you soon."

This would please her aunt. And there were a lot of things she wanted to talk over with Chad.

"Aunt Julia, cheer up and get your things together. We're going to the Willows's house to watch the races. They've got cable."

**

In the passenger's seat, Julia buckled her seatbelt and tapped the round, plastic container in her lap with her glossy red nails. "I'm so glad you thought of this. I knew there was a reason you were my favorite niece. Love you from here to the moon."

At a loss for words, all Heather could think to say was, "Right back at ya."

Julia tapped in a number on her cell. She listened and then ended the call. "Still no answer from Madam Z. Can we detour over there?"

"Maybe on the way home." Hopefully, the Derby would take her aunt's mind off the curse.

A short time later, Heather pulled into the Willows's driveway. Julia jumped out and made her way to the front door. Before she could ring the bell, Chad swung it open.

"Come in." He took the round, plastic container from Julia. "I'll heat up these pancakes. I'm starving."

Heather walked in and glanced around. She'd been in some high-priced condos in Chicago, but the furniture in this living room, with its vaulted ceiling, was more elegant than any she'd ever seen. The scent of sausages and freshly brewed coffee filled the air, along with the faint sound of an announcer's voice.

Chad waved a hand. "Come through to the kitchen."

Heather walked into an enormous, square room filled with stainless steel appliances, dark wood cabinets, and loads of counter space. Ashley sat perched on a high kitchen stool next to the stove, stirring the sausages in a large frying pan, her raven-black hair done up in pink and orchid ribbons matching the colors in her short-sleeved summer blouse.

Heather regretted not having worn something dressier than a tank top, shorts, and tennis shoes. But at least Chad matched her style of dress.

Ashley glanced up when they walked in, and a huge smile lit up her lovely face.

"Hi! I'm so glad you came today."

Heather walked over and gave her a hug. "Thanks for inviting us."

Julia followed and kissed Ashley's cheek. "How pretty you're dressed this morning. Are you ready for Derby Day?"

"Sure am," Ashley said. "It's going to be much more fun with you here. Can't wait for the first race to start."

"I'm chomping at the bit," Julia said.

"And speaking of chomping," Chad said, lifting a platter. "The pancakes are hot."

Chapter 28

HEATHER had never seen her aunt eat breakfast as swiftly as she had this morning. When she finished, she stood and walked around the kitchen, coffee cup in one hand, and a racing form in the other. "I hear an announcer, but I don't see a television. The first race starts in ten minutes."

"It's on in the den," Chad said. "Everyone grab your coffee cups, and I'll show you the way."

He led them through a short hallway and turned into the first open door. The room was much larger than the kitchen, and the overstuffed, dark brown sectional sofa appeared comfortably soft. The furniture was arranged so it wouldn't block the back yard, visible through the sliding glass door. But the most overwhelming thing about the room was the 120 inch television screen mounted to the back wall. The enormity of it was unlike anything Heather had ever seen. It was as if she was actually sitting in the stands at Churchill Downs.

"Wow!" Julia put her hands to her face. "I'll bet they don't have anything like this at the off-track betting parlor."

"You haven't been there since the remodeling," Chad said. "They have a TV just like this."

Heather wanted to ask when Chad had seen it, but she wouldn't let jealousy ruin her mood today, so she gulped down the words with the help of some warm coffee. It was amazing how Krystal managed to maneuver her way back into Chad's life after only being here a little over a week. *I'll have to keep my cool today. There's no way I can jump into a cold bath with red rose petals floating in it. At least, not while I'm here.*

Julia tapped in something on her cell phone. Heather could only assume it was her bookie's number. She sank down next to Chad on the sofa.

"Are you betting on all the races today?" he asked.

"I'm only betting on The Derby. My aunt is excellent at picking winning horses. She has it down to a science. And speaking of Aunt Julia..." Heather set her coffee cup in the cup holder next to her seat. "On the phone, you mentioned something about other charges."

A buzzer sounded on the television, and their talk was put on hold as Chad turned his head away to watch the horses gallop off in an exciting neck-and-neck race around the track.

Since Heather didn't have any money bet on the race, she didn't care what horse won, but at the end, Julia jumped out of her seat, pumped her arm, and shouted, "Yes!"

"You're so lucky," Ashley said. "The horse I picked came in fifth. Could you give me some tips?"

Julia sauntered over to Ashley's wheel chair. "Luck doesn't have much to do with picking a winning horse. Let me show you what I mean. But keep in mind, no advice is foolproof." She stooped down, and the two put their heads together in serious conversation.

"Sounds like your aunt won," Chad said.

"Kind of hard to miss. I believe you were about to tell me about the other charge pending against my aunt."

"Too many distractions in here. Let's go into the back yard. We can talk there."

Chad stood, and Heather followed him as he strolled to the sliding glass door, and they walked out. He closed it behind them and led her to the Tiki Bar next to the swimming pool.

"It's cooler here, under the awning."

Before she took a seat, she glanced into the pool. "What are those red things floating around?"

"Makki!" Chad called out.

The cat evidently thought he was being paged and sauntered over to the sliding glass door. He stood in front of it and gave out a loud *meow*.

Chad let him in and closed the door behind him.

"Makki likes to amuse himself by snatching things and dropping them into the pool. I'm always fishing stuff out. Today, it's rose petals from the garden. I think he enjoys watching them float on the water."

Madam Z said cold water with rose petals would cool my emotions. Not a bath, but close enough. Could it be a coincidence? Heather shook it off.

As if reading her thoughts, Chad asked, "It's warm enough today, would you like to go for a swim?"

This is getting spooky. "Maybe later. I've already heard about Krystal wanting to press charges for the theft of her shoes, but what else?"

Chad positioned himself on the bar stool next to her. "She's also pressing charges against your aunt for causing her bodily harm."

So he was *at the off-track betting parlor.*

"I'm my aunt's witness. Krystal tripped on her cocktail table leg as she tapped in a number on her cell phone.

The simple fact is, she wasn't paying attention to where she was going. And as far as the other shoe of hers... my aunt doesn't have it."

"So you've said. I'll talk to some people and see what I can do to help."

I know who you'll talk to, and I bet it won't be the police. But if the charges get dropped, I'm all for it.

Heather put on her most gracious smile. "Thanks."

"Now for the other thing." He went around to the back of the bar and opened the mini refrigerator. "It's sweltering out here. Would you like a cold drink?"

Despite being in the shade, droplets of sweat formed on Heather's brow. "Yes, please."

He set two bottles of Pepsi and two glasses with ice on the bar. Then he poured the cola in each glass.

Sometimes Chad says things and then leaves the words hanging. "What did you mean by 'the other thing'?"

He came around and stood in front of her. "You probably already know when they investigated the fire, they not only found it was arson, they also found charred human remains."

Heather picked up her glass and nearly choked on the effervescence. "We heard it on the news last night. My aunt freaked."

"Don't tell me she's assuming it's part of the curse?"

"She is, and since you've been honest with me, I feel the need to be honest with you. I don't care if my aunt gets upset with me. The police already know, anyway."

She told Chad about the ritual her aunt did in the field near the warehouse and how Julia had confessed to Detective Lindsey. "But we can't figure out why he let her go if she's a person of interest."

Chad sniggered. "It's because the fire was started with an accelerant, so if she gave him 'doing a ritual' with burning flowers and bark as an explanation, he probably laughed it off."

Heather dropped her shoulders in relief. "He did laugh, but why didn't he tell us?"

"He likes to keep your aunt on her toes."

"I don't understand."

"Maybe it's because of the tiff they had."

She didn't mention a tiff to me. No wonder she was giving him a hard time. "Do you know what it was about?"

"It's because he unintentionally called her Gladys while they were having dinner one evening."

"I can see why she'd be upset."

"You have to admit, she does look and dress like his ex-wife. Especially today, wearing that tight, red skirt and bright, flowered blouse. And with her hair pushed up."

"I'm sorry, but I can't admit to anything, because I've never seen his ex-wife."

"That's right, you don't know our cousin Gladys. So you'll have to take my word for it."

"But why is *he* upset with my aunt?"

"She hasn't forgiven him."

"I think she'll eventually come around." Heather leaned back in her seat and took a long sip of cola. "Have the police identified the human remains from the fire?"

"No, they don't have much to go on."

Heather put her glass on the bar. "There are too many things going on right now that don't make sense."

Chad folded his arms across his chest. "You mean like the warehouse fire?"

"And Esther's murder, one red stiletto disappearing, the unidentified human remains, and now Madam Z's gone missing."

"What do you mean *missing*?"

"My aunt's been trying to contact her. There's no answer on her phone. Nor is she answering her door, and her studio's closed down."

"Have you reported it to the police?"

"Officer Henderson knows. But Madam Z may have left town on her own." Heather reached into her shorts pocket and pulled out a folded sheet of paper.

"Then there's this."

Chapter 29

CHAD's eyes widened in a questioning look. "A train schedule?"

Heather wanted to tell him about her aunt finding it on Madam Z's printer, but before she could explain, Julia pushed the glass door aside.

"Hurry up and come in. The next race is about to start."

Heather exchanged glances with Chad. "We'll talk later."

He put his hand out in invitation. "Shall we?"

***

At the end of the race, Julia pumped her arm up and down indicating her horse had won again, but this time Ashley did too.

Chad leaned over, gazed into Heather's eyes, and gave her the open smile that always warmed her heart. "I'm glad to see Ash's having some fun. She hardly ever wins on the races."

"Maybe with my aunt around, her luck will change."

"Knowing Julia, I'm sure it will. But all kidding aside, I couldn't keep my mind on the race after everything you told me. Do you believe there's a connection between all the events you mentioned?"

"I do." Heather thought about not telling him they'd been in Esther's apartment, but he'd probably find out soon anyway. "And there's one other thing, but you have to promise, on your P.I. honor, you won't tell the police."

Chad squinted his eyes at her as if he couldn't believe she asked him to promise. "On my P.I. honor." He stood and extended his hand

She shook it. "Is there someplace private we can talk?"

Chad led her down the hall into a wood-paneled room with tall windows and a huge desk filled with electronic equipment. He touched a key on the board, and three, fifty-five inch monitors lit up.

"Welcome to my dad's world."

"Guess your family doesn't believe in doing anything on a small scale. I thought you said he lives in Florida."

"He does. But since I'm home now, he's trying to get me involved in his real estate holdings here. He wanted me to go into real estate finance after college. And there was a time when I seriously considered it." Looking down, he turned away. "But I woke up one morning and realized it wasn't for me."

About the time you broke off your engagement to Krystal? "So, you'd rather be a private investigator and a book store proprietor?"

He rubbed his clean-shaven jaw. "You know... I would. But I let my dad down once before, so I promised him I'd give it another try. And since my P.I. license is lapsed, it gives me something else to do, besides selling books."

He typed on his keyboard. "What do you want to talk to me about that you don't want the police to know?"

She hesitated a moment. *Nothing ventured...* "My aunt and I were in Esther's apartment at the retirement village yesterday afternoon. Esther had a voice mail on her phone from the Willows Bend Real Estate agency. And then I found this in a false bottom of a desk drawer."

She showed him photos of the document on her cell.

Chad stood with his mouth open as he inspected it. "You broke into Esther's apartment?"

"My aunt borrowed a key."

"No wonder you don't want me to tell the police. Don't worry. Your secret's safe with me. But now you have me curious." Chad gazed into her eyes. "You have the strangest way of doing that."

Transfixed by his warm gaze for a second, she finally turned away and emailed him the photos. "It's an old document, as you can see from the faded brown paper and the crinkled edges."

He opened his mail and studied it. "It appears to be a grant for land in this area. My dad told me the government used to issue them. After World War II, my great-granddad and a few of his military buddies procured land grants from the government to farm this area. Eventually, they were all able to buy their granted land, and some who weren't doing well sold their land to my great-granddad. He and my granddad eventually developed this town. At one time, they owned everything in it. But there might have been some land they failed to acquire."

Heather watched as Chad did a public records search.

"Esther's grandfather may, or may not, have sold the land to my great granddad. I'll see if I can access the official government records. But if this grant is a valid document, she may have owned a portion of the woods along with the land surrounding it, and the entire block of 7000 West Seventh Avenue.

"But that's where Madam Z and the Vendeglo Restaurant are located. I assumed both of their families owned those properties."

Ashley rolled her wheelchair into the room. "Thought I'd take a break from the races to get us something cool to drink. What are you two doing in here?"

Heather caught Chad's glance. "Talking."

"Is it serious?" She rolled up to the computer screen. "What's that?"

"It's a Land Grant," Chad said.

"Like the one great-granddad had from the government? Is that his grant?"

"No, it was Esther's."

Julia strolled in. "Are you talking about this?" She pulled the document out of her purse.

Heather gasped. "I thought you put that back in Esther's desk."

"I didn't have a chance. I'll do it Monday morning."

Chad accepted the document from Julia. "You should tell the police about this."

"And have them know we were snooping in Esther's apartment? Let them find it on their own."

Chad handed it back. "You're right. It might be better if they did."

Julia put the document in her purse as Christine walked in, holding a plate piled high with sandwiches wrapped in clear plastic.

"Here you are. I hope I'm not interrupting. The sliding glass door in the den was open. I brought over some ham sandwiches and potato salad for your Derby Day lunch."

Chad took the plate and container from her. "Thanks. That was considerate of you. I'll put these in the fridge, and we can eat lunch a little later." He left the room.

Julia pursed her lips. "I thought you said George was home."

"He's still sleeping. I can't wake him. We were supposed to be at the off-track betting parlor this morning, but I doubt that's ever gonna happen. We've already missed the morning races."

Ashley moved her wheel chair toward the door. "Would you like to stay and watch the rest of the races with us?"

Christine rubbed her hands together with excitement. "I was hoping you'd ask."

"Hurry up." Julia took Christine's arm and checked her watch. "The next race is about to start."

On leaving the room, Heather met up with Chad coming back from the kitchen. "Can I talk to you alone for another minute?"

"Sure. What's the problem?"

"I have this horrible feeling my aunt's going to talk Christine into going over to Madam Z's later tonight."

He cocked his head in a curious way. "Why?"

"She's convinced she can get a secret spell to eradicate her curse from one of Madam's books."

"But how would she know which one?"

"It's the thin book with a black cover, gold tipped pages and gold lettering. We both saw it. My aunt assumes it's a book of magic spells, elixirs, and invocations. She may go so far as to, what she considers, borrow it. She's more determined than ever. Especially since an unknown person was found dead in the warehouse fire, and the madam is now missing."

"You'll have to keep an eye on her tonight."

"I can't watch everything she does. Officer Henderson has already cautioned her and Christine about trying to break into Madam Z's again. I was hoping you could help."

Chad's lips lifted in a conspiratorial smile. "If I can. What do you want me to do?"

"A bit of surveillance work. I'll watch my aunt, but I'd appreciate it if you could give me a call if, or when, you see Christine's car leave her driveway tonight. Then if I can't stop my aunt, at least I'll know where they're going, and I can follow them."

"I'm a light sleeper. It's not hard to hear the Talan's car leaving their driveway. My bedroom's on that side of the house."

"Thanks. I feel so much better." Heather's stomach rumbled. "Now, did someone say something about lunch?"

Chapter 30

In the kitchen, Christine took the ham sandwich plate and the potato salad container out of the refrigerator and put them on the counter. Chad set out potato chips along with the usual condiments.

"Help yourselves," he said. "Paper plates are on the counter."

After they loaded their plates with food, Julia guided Christine to sit next to her at the table. Christine took a bite of her sandwich, but before Julia touched hers, she pulled out the folded document. "Did you know Esther had this?"

Christine put her sandwich down and took the document. "You mean this land grant? Sure, I knew." She handed the document back to Julia. "Gossip around town is she was desperate for money. Maybe she intended to sell the land. She told me about a meeting with a land developer from Chicago that was scheduled on the day she died."

"That's a lot of land," Heather said. "I'm sure the Vendeglo brothers wouldn't be thrilled about Esther selling their livelihood right out from under them. At least, that's the impression I got from Sandy. He loves that restaurant."

Chad raised an eyebrow. "How do you know how he feels about it?"

"He told me."

Chad's other eyebrow shot up. "Could one of the brothers or both have been desperate enough to kill Esther to stop the sale?"

Ashley flung an empty paper plate at her bother. "Miklos couldn't kill anyone!" She folded her arms across her chest. "I invited him over later. You can ask him how he feels about the restaurant then."

Chad rubbed his forehead "Terrific. Should I also ask him if he killed Mrs. Kwinn?"

Ashley pressed her hands on her hips. "You do, and I'll never speak to you again!"

"You don't know what he's capable of."

To stop the argument starting between brother and sister, Heather said, "It appears Esther was also selling Madam Z's business, along with her longtime residence."

"Don't start on her," Julia said. "She doesn't kill people. She tries to bring them *back* from the dead."

"She does what?" Chad's eyebrows rose.

Ashley's jaw dropped.

Heather had heard enough about that subject from the retirement village residents. "Some people in town believe she was doing occult rituals designed to bring your grandfather back from the dead, but I wouldn't put any credence in that kind of gossip."

Ashley glanced at her brother. "She can't do that without our permission, can she?"

"I guess Madam Z can do whatever she wants as long as someone's paying her, and it appears Esther was financing it with money she didn't have."

"You don't know what kind of powers the madam possesses." Christine leaned in closer. "I hear she's phenomenal."

Heather couldn't believe this. "She doesn't have any more powers than Makki does."

The cat climbed onto Ashley's shoulder. She fed him a morsel of ham as Heather patted his head. "The only *power* Madam Z has is the *power of suggestion*. And she's extremely adept at it."

"I agree with Heather," Chad said. "It's ridiculous to believe anything else."

Julia stared into the cat's eyes. "Makki must have some kind of powers. After all, he did make my red stiletto sandal disappear."

Heather let out a breath of frustration. "It has to be around the apartment somewhere. It couldn't just vanish into thin air."

The kitchen door opened. George popped his head in. "Christine, I thought I'd find you here. Come home. I'm waitin' for my lunch."

Christine put a hand to the side of her mouth and whispered, "He finally woke up."

Chad motioned toward the counter. "We have plenty of food. Grab a sandwich and whatever else you'd like to eat, and join us."

"Thanks," George came in, closing the kitchen door behind him.

"I made your favorite potato salad." Christine sounded cajoling as she jumped up and headed for the counter. "Sit at the table, and I'll put your lunch together."

"Remember, don't let the potato salad touch anything. Better yet, put it on a separate plate."

"I know," Christine said in a dismissive tone.

George put his hand up as he took the seat next to Julia. "Get me a brew too. So, what are you all talking about? I'm assuming it's the races, since The Derby's today."

Julia wiped her lips with a napkin. "Actually, we're talking about something completely different."

Christine shoved a cold beer into George's hand. "I told you about Esther Kwinn's murder and then the fire and Madam Z disappearing."

George opened the can. "Yeah, poor Esther. I didn't know her as well as Christine, but I knew about her money troubles. She was almost fifty thousand in debt to the bookies. Tried to borrow some money from me, as if I'd ever loan her any with her reputation for playing the horses. She couldn't keep away from the off-track betting parlor."

Julia nodded. "It's a hard addiction to beat."

I'm sure you know all about that. Although her aunt didn't consider her own penchant for horse racing an addiction.

"She may have borrowed money from my granddad," Chad said. "But I haven't been in town for the last five years, so I wouldn't know."

Heather thought about the man ransacking Esther's apartment. "Could she have borrowed money from her first husband? Some of the people at the retirement village said they heard her arguing with him."

George's eyes widened. "You talking about a short guy, white hair, smokes like a chimney?"

"You know him?"

"Not really. They were already divorced when she moved in next door to us. But from what I remember, the marriage was extremely troubled. He's been in and out of prison since he was a teen." George turned to Chad. "I believe he used to do odd jobs for your grandfather."

Chad took his paper plate to the counter and loaded on another sandwich. "Granddad was great for giving work to the less fortunate."

"That must be why the man was so upset when I told him your grandfather had passed away," Heather said. "He was probably hoping to get a job."

George lifted his fork. "I think he might be related to Madam Z. By the way, did you see the monstrosity of a statue she put up in the forest behind her building?"

"You mean the giant gargoyle?" Heather asked. "Yes, we've seen it."

George narrowed his eyes. "We all know about those rituals she holds back there. I don't trust her. Something hasn't been right about that woman ever since the *incident*."

"What incident?" Heather asked. This conversation was proving to be more informative than she'd imagined.

Christine set George's lunch on the table. "Don't listen to him."

"Men don't just disappear without a trace."

Christine clicked her tongue. "He didn't disappear. He left her."

George's eyes rolled in an arc. "That's what she told everyone."

Unable to restrain her curiosity, Heather asked. "What happened?"

Christine gave George a scathing glance. "Eight years ago, Madam Z's long-time husband, Nick Zancig, left town. Some say he ran off with another woman. Others say he wanted to get away from her occult rituals. Anyway, one morning she woke up, and he was gone. For years she tried to find him, even hired private investigators."

"Or so she said," George interrupted.

Christine glared at him. "She finally got word he'd fallen off a friend's boat while sailing on Lake Michigan. But his body was never recovered. So she waited for seven years, and when she still couldn't find him, she had the man declared legally dead."

George tipped his head. "That's when she cashed in his insurance policy. Does that sound suspicious, or what?"

Julia leapt out of her seat, crushed her paper plate and tossed it in the trash can. Placing a hand to her ear, she said, "I hear the next race starting. If you'll excuse me." She rushed out of the kitchen.

George grabbed his plate and stood. "Do you mind if I watch the races too?"

"Be my guest." Chad nodded. "But be careful what you say to Julia about Madam Z."

Chapter 31

THE afternoon passed quickly, and before Heather realized what time it was, the Kentucky Derby was about to start. She'd been so busy talking with everyone, she'd failed to put money on any of the horses.

"Aunt Julia, what are the odds on Fatal again?"

Julia checked out the racing board. "They're thirty to one now. Why?"

"Is it too late to contact your bookie? I'd like to put money on your horse."

Julia grabbed her cell phone. "How much do you want to bet?"

"Fifty." It was more than she could spare at the moment, but like her aunt always said, sometimes you had to take a chance.

"I'll contact him. He'll do it for me."

Heather let out a sigh of relief. Her winnings would help a great deal toward her expenses. She'd have to get a job soon or file bankruptcy. Her dreams of having an online marketing business would have to be put on hold for a while. Or at least until she could figure out a way to get it up and running.

As the buzzer went off, indicating the start of the big race, Heather slid the glass door open and walked outside to stand by the pool. She couldn't watch. If her horse lost, the disappointment would be overwhelming.

A while later, Chad came out.

"Sorry to tell you, but your horse didn't win."

"What am I going to do now?"

Chad placed a comforting hand on her shoulder. "It sounds like your winnings would have been the most important thing in your life at the moment."

"Moneywise? They would have been."

"I thought you were setting up an online marketing business."

"I did, but it's a slow start. It takes time and advertising money to get it to where I'd actually be able to draw a salary. And I don't know how long that will take, especially since my former boss has spread some nasty, and untrue, rumors about me throughout the marketing sector. It seems like I'm a poor business risk, and none of my former clients will talk to me, much less hire me."

"Maybe you should go into another line of work."

"You mean like being a sales clerk in one of the boutique shops in lovely downtown Willows Bend?" The words came out with more sarcasm than she'd intended.

Chad's eyebrows rose. "What's wrong with that? I do it."

"Yes, but the difference is, you own the store. Besides, I'm a little over-qualified for a sales position. And my aunt and I are leaving town when her community service sentence has ended."

Chad's lips dipped into a frown. "If I hear of anything you're not *over-qualified* for, and can do in the short term, I'll let you know."

Is he offended? Her words sometimes did offend people, but it was always unintentional. *Why can't I keep my mouth shut?*

"Sorry about your horse." He swung around and marched back into the house.

Heather couldn't stand the thought of him being angry with her. She rushed in after him. He retreated to the kitchen. She couldn't keep up, but she did run into her aunt, which annoyed her just as much. "I thought you said Fatal was going to win the Derby?"

"No. What I said was, I would bet your fifty. I didn't say I was going to bet it on Fatal to *win*. I wouldn't bet on the nose of a horse I wasn't sure of, so I bet it to *show*, like I did for the folks at the retirement village. And he showed! So smile. You're still in for some money, honey."

Heather let out a breath somewhere between joy and relief. "Thanks. I should have known you'd come through for me." She headed toward the kitchen.

"Where're you going?"

She didn't want to tell her aunt she'd had a disagreement with Chad. "I'm getting a glass of water."

As she entered the kitchen, Chad slipped his barbecue apron on. Whatever he was angry about, she had to fix it before she left today.

"Since the Derby's over, my aunt and I will be going home. By the way, I still won some money on my horse."

He opened the double doors on the huge, stainless steel refrigerator and searched the shelves. "I'm happy for you."

Why doesn't he sound happy? "I hope I didn't offend you with what I said outside."

He turned to her, his face impassive. "I'm not offended."

She watched for any indication he might be lying. "I'm glad, because it didn't mean anything."

His eyes flashed. "I wish you wouldn't go."

Her heart flipped. She wasn't sure how to take those words. Did he mean don't go now, or when her aunt finished her community service sentence?

He pulled out a box of pre-made hamburgers. "Since you brought breakfast, and the Talan's supplied us with lunch, I thought I'd throw some burgers on the grill."

He must mean now. "Sure. We'd love to stay. How can I help?"

"I'll take these outside, and you can let the others know we've moved the party to the back yard."

***

As Chad busied himself with lighting the grill, Ashley and Christine brought out the buns and the condiments. Heather emptied potato chips into several large bowls on the picnic table. Julia accompanied George to the bar. He chose another beer from the fridge and offered his companion one.

"Thanks." Julia popped open the top. She took a sip as she walked toward Heather, lifting the can to show her.

"Forget the beer," Ashley said. "We're drinking bubbly to celebrate Julia helping me win money betting on The Derby." She wheeled herself onto the concrete patio with a magnum in her lap, as Makki, tail pointed up, trailed behind.

Chad rushed to her side and grabbed the huge bottle. "Let me take this. It's heavy." Makki climbed into Ashley's, now empty, lap.

Chad walked the bottle to the bar and handed it to George. "Do you mind helping out with this?"

George set his beer can down. "Not at all. I'll get the flutes."

Chad headed to the grill.

Officer Henderson strolled into the yard in a pale blue sports shirt and black Bermuda shorts. "I hope I'm not late."

"No, you're right on time," Chad said. "Grab something to drink. I haven't put the burgers on the flame yet."

There were more footsteps on the cement walk, and a few moments later, Vikki Garret, the hotel desk clerk, walked in with a bottle of red wine in her hand.

Heather's heart sank. *Who invited her?*

Christine rushed up to Vikki. "I'm so glad you could make it."

Vikki grinned. "Thanks for inviting me. I can't tell you how long I've been waiting to get close to a certain person." She motioned toward Chad with the wine bottle and then handed it to Christine.

"I know. You've told me often enough."

Heather couldn't help but overhear their conversation as she stood a couple of feet away. *I hope it's not going to be one of those evenings where I have to vie for Chad's attention.* She meandered over to George. "Have you poured the Champagne yet?"

He handed her a tall flute, filled to the top. She took a sip as Christine and Vikki came up behind her.

Vikki accepted a flute from George. "What are you celebrating?"

"Ashley's win on the Kentucky Derby today."

"She's so lucky. I didn't get a chance to bet this year." Vikki giggled. "But then I always lose, so what's the point? I'm just unlucky."

"Luck had nothing to do with it," Julia said. "I showed her the finer points of betting to give her better odds of winning."

Officer Henderson, who'd been talking to Chad as he grilled the burgers, made his way to the bar. He accepted a champagne flute from George.

Ashley rolled her chair near them with the cat curled up in her lap. Her nervous fingers tapped on her cell phone. "It's getting late. I wonder what happened to Miklos? He should have been here by now. I just texted him, but he didn't answer. I hope nothing's wrong at the restaurant."

"From what I've heard, they're pretty busy today," Officer Henderson said. "He probably couldn't get away. If you want, I'll take a ride over to check things out."

"It's kind of you. But I'm sure you're right. He's probably just busy." Makki gave out a quiet meow, as if to reassure her.

A cell phone buzzed. Everyone checked theirs.

"It's mine." Ashley read the text out loud. "Too busy now. I'll try to make it later. Smiley face." She put the phone over her heart. "At least I know."

Makki sniffed the air, jumped off her lap, and scampered toward the grill.

"I can't keep up with that cat." Ashley put her flute down and raced after him.

"Miklos is busy is all right," Vikki said. "And I know who he's busy with."

"What do you mean?" Christine asked.

"I don't know why Ashley bothers with him. She could find someone much better suited to her."

Heather couldn't help but overhear. *Sounds like the green-eyed monster is rearing its ugly head.*

Christine shook a finger at Vikki. "Ashley's a lovely young woman, but at the moment she doesn't think much of herself. Once she gets her confidence back, she'll see him for what he truly is."

Chapter 32

HEATHER was the last to get her burger. She settled herself at the end of the picnic table, hoping Chad would choose to sit next to her. Vikki grabbed her plate and came around to seat herself next to Heather, so Chad would have no other place to sit but next to *her*.

Chad grabbed his plate, pulled up a lawn chair and stationed it three feet from everyone. Satisfied he wasn't next to Vikki, Heather took a bite and had to admit, the man certainly knew how to grill. This was the juiciest and tastiest burger she'd had in a long time.

Crickets chirped, and lightning bugs flashed near the flower garden, but no one spoke as they ate.

George broke the silence. "Your burgers are great, Chad. I could eat another one."

Christine jumped up. "I'll get it for you, George." Leaving the half-eaten burger on her plate, she headed to the grill.

"And another brew," George called after her as he settled himself back at the table. "So, Henderson, how's the investigation into Esther Kwinn's murder coming along? Got any suspects?"

Henderson pinched the bridge of his nose. "I can't talk about the case."

"Why not? We're all friends here. Unless you suspect one of us is the murderer."

"I can't say."

"So, you do." George glanced around the table. "You can eliminate me. I was out of town when the murder took place, and you can eliminate my wife. Christine had no reason to kill Esther. Besides, she's not the type to kill anyone."

"When it comes to murder, there is no type. There's only motive," Henderson said.

Christine slammed the plate in front of George. "Well, then I had no motive." She crossed her arms.

"I'm sorry if my observation offended you, Mrs. Talan. I only meant it as a generalization."

"Well then, who *does* have a motive?" Christine asked.

"How about her ex-husband?" The words poured from Heather's lips before she could stop them.

Henderson glanced her way. "Why would *he* want her dead?"

"I don't know. What was he looking for in her apartment at the retirement village when he ransacked the place?" Relief flushed through her. She needed to let the police know about this but didn't know how to do it without implicating herself or her aunt.

Henderson stood. "How would you know?"

"I um... drove there to check on my aunt who was at the retirement village doing community service. But when I got there, I noticed that Esther's door was open, and an elderly man, whom I found out later was her ex, was ripping through her things." *There, now he knows.*

"Why didn't you come to the police with this information?"

Heather glanced at her aunt. "We went to the station to talk to Detective Lindsey that afternoon."

"But his high and mightiness," Julia jumped in, "was so involved with the fire and those red stiletto sandals, he didn't give Heather a chance to say anything."

"I'm not surprised. With two murders and an arson, he's overwhelmed.

"Did anyone claim Esther's body for burial?" Chad asked.

"Yeah, the gray-haired man in the brown bomber jacket who identified her."

Christine picked up her plate and headed toward the trash can. "You don't suppose Esther considered her ex as the evil entity she said she was being followed by. I mean, did she even know he was back in town?"

"She must have," Heather said. "As I told you earlier, some seniors at the retirement village heard her arguing with him. It could have been over money."

"That's always a first-rate motive," Officer Henderson said. "But there could be others we don't know about."

Chad waved a hand in front of his face to shoo a bug away. "The mosquitoes are out, and it's getting dark. I'll light some Tiki Torches."

George rose from the table. "I'll help. Get me another beer, Christine."

"In a minute."

Is that sarcasm in Christine's voice? Heather wouldn't have been surprised from the way George had ordered her around all day. If it was her, she would've rebelled long before this.

Chad shoved the torches around the patio area and then lit them, while George brought out enough lawn chairs for everyone. Officer Henderson opened a chair for Julia.

She grabbed his muscular arm as she lowered herself into it. "Have you found out if Madam Z has returned, yet?"

"I've been stationed at the off-track betting parlor since early this morning, so I haven't had a chance to check. Why don't you try calling her?"

"I did. No answer, and her voice mail is full. She could be being held somewhere against her will."

"By whom?"

"If I knew who, I'd probably know where. She could be locked in a closet or tied up in her own basement... maybe even dead."

He turned to Christine. "We all checked the house last night, and she wasn't there. But she was warned not to leave town. So, if she's taken off somewhere, we *will* find her."

Julia raised an eyebrow. "Are you telling me you reported her missing?"

"I filled out a missing person's report."

"But if she knows not to leave, she may still be here."

"You found a train schedule she printed out." Heather said. "Why would she print one if she didn't intend to leave?"

Hands on his hips, Office Henderson glared at Julia. "Where did you find it?"

"On her printer," Julia admitted.

"You should've given it to me."

Julia's eyes blinked. "You know about it now."

"This could put a new spin on things."

Chad laughed. "You have to admit, Julia's pretty resourceful."

"Yeah, I'd say sneaky was more like it."

"I've been thinking," Julia said. "If she left town, why didn't she take the train schedule with her?"

Christine sauntered over to them. "Because someone wants us to *think* she left town. We should check her basement and her attic the next time."

George glared at his wife. "What were you up to while I was on the road?"

Christine gave him a dismissive glance.

Henderson moved between the ladies. "Don't you two go near the place."

"Well, of course we're not going there alone.," Julia said with a pleading smile. "In light of what I told you, you're coming with us, aren't you?"

"She's got you there," Chad said.

Heather tsked. "Aunt Julia, would you kindly leave the officer alone and let him do his job?"

"He's knows I'm going to get there one way or another. So he might as well give in right now." She turned to face him. "What do you say?"

Officer Henderson rubbed his forehead. "If you feel so strongly about it, I'll make a deal with you. I'll put in for a court order to search the place."

Julia paced in front of him. "Not acceptable. That'll take too much time. She could be dying as we speak."

Henderson lifted his arms up and dropped them to his side. "What am I going to do with you two?" He plopped into a lawn chair.

"Don't be too hard on the ladies," Chad said. "They're only trying to help."

"By hiding evidence and lying about it?"

"But I'm showing and telling you now," Julia said. "Doesn't that count for something?"

"I guess so," he said. "But if you'd have done it sooner, we might have gotten somewhere."

George wandered over to Officer Henderson. "I'll tell you what I think."

"We're all ears," Christine said, sarcasm dripping from every word.

Ignoring her, George took a sip from his beer can and glanced around as if to make sure everyone was listening. "I think Madam Z killed Esther Kwinn because Esther was going to sell her livelihood, and her home, to a developer."

"But she could always move to another empty storefront," Julia argued. "There are several of them in town."

"I'm going to play Devil's advocate." George pointed at Christine in case she might make a sly remark about him working with the Devil.

She made a zipping motion across her lips.

"What if..." George continued, "and this is only speculation, but what if there's something either in her house or buried on the grounds, she doesn't want anyone to find?"

"You don't know what you're talking about." Julia waved her hand at him. "From all the mystery programs I've watched on television, the guilty person is not always the most likely suspect. Who else knew Esther was going to be in the park at that time of the morning, besides Madam Z?"

Christine walked over to George and collected a couple of empty beer cans. "It's common knowledge the seniors from the retirement village have a water aerobics class from seven-thirty to nine on Thursday mornings. Esther was a member. They arrive at the park field house at seven. It's kind of early, so some of them go for a short walk around the park to limber up. And Esther was one of the usual walkers."

"Narrows it down to everyone in the retirement village." Henderson said. "But who among them had a motive?"

Heather didn't say anything and hoped no one else would, either. This kind of talk only encouraged her aunt to do more investigating. And the worst part was she wouldn't be able to stop her.

Chapter 33

MIKLOS strolled into the yard. "Hi, everyone."
Ashley rolled up to him, a huge smile on her face. "I'm glad you made it."

"Hello, gorgeous."

His standard line. But I'm sure Ashley never gets tired of hearing it.

She beamed at him. "We're about to have dessert. I had the bakery make a special Kentucky Derby cake, in the shape of a derby hat. And we have three flavors of ice cream."

"I can't stay long. I'll eat, and then I have to get back to the restaurant. My brother's expecting me to relieve him at the reservations desk."

Chad stood. "Guess I'll make coffee."

Vikki jumped out of her chair. "I'll be glad to help."

Christine got up and headed toward the kitchen. "No, you two stay out here and talk. I know where everything is. I'll take out the ice cream, slice the cake, and let you know when the coffee's ready."

"Thanks, that's kind of you." Chad leaned back in his lawn chair.

To Heather's dismay, Vikki pulled a chair up next to him. She should pull up a chair on his other side, but that reeked of desperation. She'd just keep an eye on them.

"You and your brother must love the restaurant," Julia said to Miklos. "Sounds like you spend a lot of time there."

Miklos huffed. "My brother does. He'd do anything to keep it. But I don't. I want to be an architect, not a restaurateur. And as soon as I get enough money together, I'm out of there."

"I thought the restaurant was doing a first-rate business." Julia said.

"You'd think so, wouldn't you? But with the turnover in staff, constantly losing silverware, broken dishes and glassware, and trying to please disgruntled customers, it's a hassle. We can't even get decent kitchen help. No one wants to wash dishes these days." He rubbed his handsome chin. "Except that elderly man who came in a couple of days ago, asking for a job."

Could it be? "Did he smoke and wear a brown bomber jacket?" Heather asked.

"Yeah, that's him. At first I was skeptical. He looked like another vagrant. We've hired those before, but they're not reliable. My brother told me Madam Z said to trust this guy, so we hired him."

Julia glared at her niece. "She told me to trust him too."

Heather turned from her aunt to Miklos. "Does Madam Z have a lot to say in the way you run your restaurant?"

"Sandy goes to her for advice. I don't know what kind of hold she has over him, but it seems to get stronger every year."

Officer Henderson cleared his throat. "Miklos, did you notice if Madam Z was back, before you came here?"

"I didn't even know she was gone."

"According to your brother," Heather said, "she often goes away for a few days at a time."

"I don't pay attention to what she does. But I did see a light in her basement window as I was driving out of the parking lot. Of course, it might have only been the reflection of the setting sun on the glass."

Julia pulled Heather to the side. "I told you something was going on there."

A moment later, Christine opened the kitchen door. "Coffee and dessert, anyone?"

Although everything looked yummy, Heather opted for coffee only, as everyone headed toward the cake and ice cream on the counter. Although she was still slim, eating take-out food for most of her meals these days was putting on pounds in places she didn't need them. Time for some healthy cooking classes, or she'd have to stop eating dessert altogether.

Miklos scarfed down his cake and coffee. "It's getting late. Sandy's going to kill me if I don't get back like... " He checked his cell phone. "Right now. Thanks for inviting me over, Ashley."

"Couldn't you stay a little longer?"

"I'll call you later." He kissed her forehead, then headed out the kitchen door.

Officer Henderson yawned. "I'll be going too. I'm on duty tomorrow morning." He placed his paper plate in the trash and put his coffee cup in the sink. "But before I leave..." He turned to Julia. "I don't want you or Christine to go anywhere near Madam Z's place tonight. If something did happen to her, you could get hurt."

"You don't have to worry about Christine," George said. "She's not going anywhere tonight, except home."

Christine stuck her tongue out behind her husband's back.

Henderson shook Chad's hand. "Thanks for dinner."

"You're welcome." Chad said.

"Before you leave." Heather caught the officer's attention. "I think you should question Bax about Madam Z's husband's disappearance."

"That was a long time ago. What does it have to do with Esther's murder?"

"Bax may know something. When he was married to Esther, they might have all been friends. Maybe he knows what really happened to Madam Z's husband. Esther may have known too, but vowed not to say anything."

Henderson's eyebrows scrunched. "Then why bring it up now?"

"Esther needed money. She could have been blackmailing Madam Z."

"I'll mention it to Detective Lindsey."

Vikki took her plate to the trash and refilled her coffee cup. "Bax is a pretty tough character. You might not get anything out of him."

Heather's jaw dropped. "When I asked you about him at the hotel, you said you didn't know the man."

"No. You asked if he had checked into the hotel. And I said he hadn't on my shift. But I never said I didn't know him."

"How?" Henderson asked.

"When I was a little girl, he used to visit my grandfather. I never found out why they were friends, but I overheard my grandparents talking about my gramps visiting him in prison."

Henderson fingered the screen on his cell. "We've already checked him out. He's got a log rap sheet. Mostly passing bad checks, forgery, theft, and larceny, but nothing close to murder."

"Maybe he's moved up in the world of crime," Julia suggested.

"I'd like to be present when you question him," Chad said.

"I don't see why that would be a problem if Lindsey okays it."

Heather motioned Chad to follow her outside. After he closed the kitchen door behind him, she whispered, "Would you see if you can find out why he was ransacking Esther's apartment?"

He pinned her with his eyes and leaned in closer. "I'll see what I can do. And by the way…"

Passion stirred her insides. "Yes?"

His gaze softened. "Do you know your green eyes twinkle like highly polished emeralds when you get excited?"

Heat rushed to Heather's face. *Why does he say things like that to me?* Her lips parted, but before she could speak, the kitchen door swung open, and Vikki sandwiched herself between them.

"What are you two talking about out here?"

Chad took a few steps back, the half-smile on his lips suggesting a hint of embarrassment. "It's a secret."

Her gaze shifted from him to Heather. "We've been friends all our lives. I didn't think we had any secrets."

"You have no idea." He winked at Heather and walked back into the kitchen.

Vikki's mouth fell open as her eyes blazed with jealousy.

That look would have withered a weaker woman. Heather grinned with satisfaction.

Chapter 34

HEATHER tossed and turned in bed that night, trying to find a comfortable position, she couldn't shake the warmth she felt when Chad leaned in close and mentioned her twinkling, emerald eyes.

It took a while before her mind finally settled down enough for her to fall asleep. And the moment she did, her cell phone rang. She turned over and picked it up. "Hello," she said in a sleepy, dream-like voice.

"Hi, it's Chad."

Heather's eyelids shot open. She remembered why she asked him to call her. "Did Christine's car leave their driveway?"

"It has. What's the plan now?"

"What time is it?"

"A little after one."

"I don't know where Christine's going, but I'm pretty sure my aunt's asleep. I'd better check."

Heather swung her legs over the side of the bed and stepped into her slippers. She turned her aunt's doorknob and peeked in. Julia's bed was messy, but she wasn't in it. Heather ran to the living room window and gazed at the street below.

Julia was clearly visible on the sidewalk under the streetlamp. Heather pulled up the sash and stuck her head out. "Aunt Julia, you'd better not be going to Madam Z's."

Julia looked up and waved as Christine's car pulled up next to her. She got in and they turned onto 7th Avenue.

Heather closed the window and put the phone to her ear.

"It's too late, they're on their way to Madam Z's studio right now. I don't know how they're getting in, but I can imagine my aunt picking the lock on the back door. I'd better go there and try to talk some sense into her."

"Good luck, and be careful. You don't know what's going on out there."

"Thanks. I'm always careful from years of living in the city." She said the words with more confidence than she felt.

She'd had to park her car a block away last night, and now she dreaded walking the streets alone, especially with all the strangers in town for Derby weekend. But she had to stop her aunt before the police caught up with her again.

***

Heather pulled her car up to the front of the Vende-glo restaurant, but parked up the street in case a patrol car drove by and the police wondered what it was doing there. She made her way around the back of the long, brick building. The restaurant had an alarm system light on. It was dim on this pitch-black, moonless night, but at least it was enough light to see where she was. Her flashlight afforded her a little more help.

Pressing herself against the back wall of the restaurant, Heather tip-toed her way to Madam Z's studio, where she spotted Christine's car in the woods.

They weren't inside. *Maybe they're in the house.* Backing away from the car, her arm touched something solid. Heart pounding, Heather swung around with her flashlight in hand. The gargoyle's hideous face blazed in the bright light like some ferocious monster. Ready to scream, she realized what it was.

"It's only you." Turning away, she let out a long breath. "What an ugly thing."

"What are you doing here?" A sharp, high-pitched voice asked from behind.

Heather tensed a moment and turned her head. Madam Z stood beside her, wearing a long, black robe like the last time Heather had seen her. She carried a dim lantern and held it near her face. In the darkness, she appeared to be a floating white head.

"You scared me." *Think fast.* She rubbed her eyes and yawned. "I don't know what I'm doing here either. I must be sleepwalking."

"I knew you were exceedingly troubled."

Heather couldn't hold her frustration in any longer. "Where have you been? My aunt's frantic at not being able to find you. And I'm furious you left her to take the fall for starting the warehouse fire."

"I can't help it if she's the way she is."

The sad part was Heather understood what the Madam meant.

Madam Z put the lantern down. "But I was never away. The police cautioned me not to leave town."

"Your store is closed up, and no one can reach you."

"I've been living deep in the woods for the past two days. Out of the reach of man. Spring is a time of renewal, and I always restore myself in May. I pick Kentucky Derby weekend to get away from the unpleasant vibes coming from the strangers in town. I retreat into the woods before they can ask me for the winning horse. I can't give it to them. I'm not a psychic. And I wouldn't even if I could. From past experience, they can get extremely rude and demanding."

Heather flashed her light at the back door of the studio. "I guess no one ever thinks of looking for you in the woods."

I've got to find a way to let them know she's back. In case they're doing something they shouldn't be.

"So, you knew Esther's first husband, I understand."

"What an odd thing to say."

"My aunt said she'd met an older man at the restaurant the other day, and we recently found out he was married to Esther."

"I should know him. He's my brother, Baxter."

George said he could be related to her, but I never expected that connection.

The madam lowered her eyelids. "Poor Baxter has had a hard life and has been in prison from time to time. But he's on the straight and narrow now. He even has a job. What he needs is a woman like your aunt to keep him on an even keel, even though she *is* cursed. I was hoping they'd hit it off, but your aunt has more problems than even he can deal with."

She did *set my aunt up to meet him. I knew it.*

"But enough about my brother. Come walk with me in the woods. Your troubles will pass away."

"If only it was that simple," Heather murmured.

"The trees and the earth are great for grounding yourself."

Heather had never heard this. It might be another of Madam Z's made up rituals. "What do you mean?"

"Grounding is the practice of connecting to the Earth. It releases your negative energy into the ground and draws in positive energy from Mother Nature, which replenishes and recharges your whole being."

"Sounds wonderful. I could use a recharge." Heather checked her cell. "But not now. It's almost two a.m., and I have to get back before my aunt finds me gone."

Madam Z pointed to Christine's car. "Yours?"

Heather walked over to it and tried the driver's side door. It opened. *They must have planned a quick getaway.*

She pretended to rummage through her shoulder bag for the keys. "As I was sleepwalking, or sleep driving in this case, I must have dropped my keys somewhere."

She checked the ground, and then inside the car where she leaned on the horn. "Oops."

A few moments later, two figures crept around the side of the building and headed toward her, one holding a flashlight, the other some sort of weapon.

"Who's beeping the horn?" Christine cried out as she flashed her light in Heather's eyes.

She blinked and put her hand up to block the light.

"Oh, it's only you." Christine sounded relieved. "What are you doing here?"

"Trying to find you two."

Julia lowered her plastic baseball bat, and jerked her thumb toward the ground behind her. "You should see the huge herb and flower garden the madam is growing back there. It's probably where she gets all the ingredients to make her magic elixirs."

Heather turned. "Why don't you ask her yourself?" But Madam Z had disappeared.

"She was standing by the gargoyle statue a minute ago."

"Who?" Julia asked.

"Madam Z. She never left town. She's been living in the woods for the past couple of days, renewing herself."

"She's here?" Julia sounded ecstatic.

"Yes." Heather pointed. "See, she left her lantern."

Christine checked her cell phone. "As long as we know nothing's happened to her, I have to go. If George wakes up and finds me gone, there'll be 'H' to pay." She opened her car door, slid into the driver's seat, and drove away.

"Come on." Heather flashed her light toward the street. "My rental's parked down the block."

"Wait a minute." Julia turned around. "Why would Madam Z go back into the woods without her lantern?"

Chapter 35

HEATHER yawned. "You can ask her later this morning. Let's go. I'm tired."

"But I have to talk to her now. It can't wait." Julia headed for the gargoyle. Swinging her bat in one hand, she picked up the lantern with the other before Heather could stop her.

"All right, but hurry up. I'll wait here." Heather walked back to sit on the steps of the studio and turned off her flashlight. *No use wasting batteries.*

Julia headed into the woods.

A form crept toward her from the restaurant parking lot.

Heather leaned back and used the darkness as cover. She could barely make out a man's figure. Panic gripped her throat. *I need a weapon.* She glanced around, but only darkness surrounded her. She fingered the flashlight. *This will have to do. If nothing else, I can always flash it in his eyes to distract him.*

She tiptoed behind the man, keeping a distance of a few yards. His tall figure flashed between the trees and the lantern's dim light. As he got closer to her aunt, she attempted to control her rapid heartbeat with deep breathing. And then she shifted her brain into fight mode.

Heather checked her cell phone—no bars. She tried not to panic.

Julia stopped walking and stood frozen for a moment. The man mirrored her movements. She swung around with one arm behind her back.

Good thing she's got that bat.

Then Julia held up the lantern to eye level. "Who's there? Is that you, Madam Z?"

Heather ducked behind a tree and waited to see what Julia would do as the man approached her.

"No. It's me."

Julia's shoulders dropped. She obviously recognized him. "What are you doing out here at this time of night?"

"No, a better question is, what are *you* doing out here? Looking for trouble would be my guess. Always sticking your nose where it doesn't belong." Detective Lindsey's voice sounded strained.

Julia huffed. "How did you know I was here?"

"Henderson called. He was concerned you might try something foolish."

"There's no law against wandering the woods at night, is there?"

"Not if you want to get killed. Remember, there's a murderer on the loose."

Julia moved her head from side to side. "I doubt if he or she will have the same motive to kill me as they did to murder Esther. Besides, I've been in more dangerous places than this."

"You were lucky." The detective rubbed his forehead. "Honesty, Julia, you are the most exasperating woman I've ever met. Go home."

Julia let out a giggle. "Or what? You'll arrest me on some made-up charge?"

"If that's what it takes to get you safely back home."

"Don't worry, I'm going," Julia said, her voice dismissing his concern.

"It's about time." He turned to leave.

"As soon as I find Madam Z."

He swung back around. "You don't have to find her. That's our job."

Julia scrunched her nose. "You don't have to either. I heard she's been living in these woods since Friday."

He put his arms up in a gesture of surrender. "I give up. Stay here. I can't make you leave, but if something happens, don't say I didn't warn you."

He turned on his heels and marched into the darkness.

Heather came out from behind the tree and joined her aunt. "You were fortunate it was Detective Lindsey. It could have been anyone."

Julia grabbed Heather's arm as if to steady herself. "You're telling me. At first, I thought it might be the killer. My knees are still shaking." She sat on the ground.

"We can't stay here. Let's get out of the woods. You can see Madam Z in the morning." Heather put her hand under Julia's arm to help her stand. "Which way?"

"I don't know. I thought I'd catch up with her. I wasn't paying attention. Don't you know?"

"I was following you." Heather pulled out her cell phone. "I'd call someone, but this seems to be a dead spot."

"Guess that's why the madam finds it so relaxing here. No distractions."

"Yes, but she's familiar with the area and knows her way out. She might have even doubled back to her studio by now."

Julia rummaged inside her purse. "We can always start a fire and wait for the fire department to come and rescue us."

"I have a better idea. Why don't we turn around and see if we can follow the detective. If we head in the same direction, we're bound to find our way out sooner or later."

Julia glanced around. "Or get lost deeper in the woods."

"Try not to be negative."

Julia kept the lantern at eye level as they walked, until a few moments later when it died. She stopped to shake it. "What's the matter with this thing?"

"Must be out of batteries, or fuel, or whatever it uses," Heather said. "No wonder Madam Z left it. The thing's useless."

Julia put the lantern down. "Do you hear something?" she whispered.

"Only crickets and the occasional owl hooting." Heather was almost afraid to ask. "What do you hear?"

"Voices," Julia whispered. "They're coming from that direction." Julia pointed to her left, and put a finger to her lips. "Shhh."

Faint murmurings filled the night air.

"I hear them now," Heather whispered back. "Why are we whispering?"

"In case something illegal's going down. Why else would people be in the woods at this time of the morning?"

Heather stared at her aunt. "*We're* here."

"Yeah, but we're lost." Julia shivered.

Heather grabbed her aunt's arm and huddled close for warmth as they walked in the direction of the voices.

Every time they got near, the voices moved deeper into the woods, until Heather spotted two lantern lights not far from them and motioned for Julia to stop and duck behind a tree until they could get a better idea of what was going on. Her aunt might be right about whatever it was being illegal.

One man sat on the ground while the other dug near him with a shovel. "I can't believe you don't remember where you buried it."

The other man stopped. "My memory's not what it used to be. I couldn't take the chance of putting up some kind of marker."

"Then you should have made a map. Keep digging. We have to find it." He let out a congested cough and lit a cigarette.

The other man dropped to the ground. "I'm dead on my feet. Let's come back tomorrow night and try again. I know it has to be here."

"You knew it was in the last place we dug up too." They both stood and picked up their lanterns and shovels. As they walked away, their voices faded.

Heather stood glued to her spot behind the tree. Julia sauntered over to her. "You know who those guys are?" she whispered.

Heather nodded.

"I know the guy in the bomber jacket is Bax, but who's the other one?"

"That's Harry from the dry cleaners."

"How does Bax know Harry?"

"Not sure. But according to Vikki the hotel clerk, everyone knows everyone in this town via six shades of separation."

"I wonder what they were digging for."

At this point, Heather didn't care. She put a finger to her lips and motioned her aunt to come closer. "We're going to follow them out of the woods. Hopefully, without being seen or heard."

Chapter 36

THE men were only a short distance ahead, close enough to see their lantern's light but not close enough to hear what was being said. Heather's eyelids, heavy with sleep, fluttered closed a few times. She checked her phone for bars. No luck yet.

The men stopped at a black, compact sedan, got inside, and drove away.

Heather figured if they kept walking in the direction the car drove off in, they'd have to reach a point where she'd eventually get some bars on her phone.

Julia walked alongside Heather. "I've been thinking about what George suggested at dinner."

"He suggested a lot of things."

"I'm talking about someone killing Madam Z's husband so she could collect his insurance. Maybe Harry did it and then buried him in the woods. That could be what they were trying to dig up. Esther might have told Bax she intended to sell the land to a developer, in which case, they'd have to move the body."

Oh boy, here we go. "But Esther isn't selling the land anymore."

"Whoever inherits the land might. I mean, what else would they be digging up in the middle of the night?"

"You've got a crazy imagination. They could have been digging for something entirely different."

Both of their phones tweaked to life. Heather's rang. "Thank Goodness!" She checked the caller ID and put the phone to her ear. "Hi, Chad."

"Where've you been?" He sounded concerned. "I've been trying to call for the last hour. Did you turn your phone off?"

"I've been lost in the woods with my aunt, and right now we're on a lonely stretch of road in the middle of nowhere. I couldn't get bars on my phone out here."

"What type of road are you walking on?"

"Red brick."

"There's only one road left in this town that's still made of bricks, and that runs between a short stretch of the woods and the old cemetery. Stay put, and I'll come to get you."

Heather shuddered. "By a cemetery? That's a grim thought. I'd rather keep walking toward town. That way if you don't find us, we'll get there eventually."

She ended the call.

"Where's the cemetery?" Julia asked.

"It's on the other side of the street."

Julia walked to the cemetery side. She stopped and turned on the flashlight app on her phone. "I see headstones, old ones, and possibly mausoleums way back there. I'll bet this is where Madam Z's been hiding out since Friday."

"Why would she pick a cemetery?"

"It's a sure bet nobody would bother her here, especially at night. It has to be a lot easier to communicate with the dead in a cemetery. It's probably where she gets her dark, mystical, occult energy." Julia took a few steps inside the cemetery and sucked in a deep breath. "Can't you feel the power filling you up?"

Heather walked a little closer to her aunt, and shivers ran up her spine. "The only thing I feel is creepy."

"That's because you don't have a connection to it like I do. You're not the one who's plagued with a curse."

That curse again. "I don't want to be here."

Walking toward the street, Julia tripped over a low headstone and dropped to the ground.

Heather rushed over to her. "Are you hurt?"

Julia struggled to her feet, rubbed the dirt from her hands, and picked up her baseball bat. "I'm not hurt. But it was a sign! The cemetery is stopping me from leaving. Look!" She pointed to the sky. "That's the new moon."

Heather glanced up as clouds passed away, and the round, yellow orb was now visible.

"This is the time Madam Z will be able to get rid of my curse. I feel it in my gut. It has to be tonight." Julia crept between the headstones and disappeared into the darkness.

I've heard my aunt declare some crazy things, but this is the craziest. I won't be able to stop her now that she's gotten a sign. But I don't have to go along with it.

Heather checked the few bars on her cell phone and called to her aunt. "I'll wait for Chad and call you when he gets here."

She paced the brick road, goose bumps stippling her arms. The temperature had dropped a few degrees. A pair of playful squirrels chased each other along the road and around the trees. She tried to keep out of their way.

A few moments later, headlights came toward her. Excited, she waved. The car passed. Then it stopped, turned around, and came back.

That's not Chad's car. She ran deeper into the woods and jumped behind a tree, hoping the occupants hadn't seen where she went.

A familiar lantern's light came toward her. She peeked around the tree and caught her breath as her heart beat to near suffocation. The two men who'd been digging earlier came toward her, carrying their shovels.

Why did they have to come back?

They stopped walking almost in front of her. Bax waved his lantern around. "Is it here?"

"Yeah, it's right here." Harry grabbed Heather's forearm. She'd underestimated them. He pulled her from behind the tree. "I told you we were being followed."

"I don't know w-what you m-mean," Heather stammered, barely able to speak. "I'm not following you."

"Then what are you doing here at this time of the morning?"

"I... I was um... sleepwalking. I suddenly woke up in the middle of the woods, and I was trying to find my way home."

Harry grabbed the phone from her back pocket. "Do you always sleep with your cell?"

"I must have unconsciously put it in my pocket. Force of habit."

"Do you believe her?" Harry asked.

"Not for a minute." Bax lit a cigarette. "She hangs out with Willows's grandson. He's been sticking his nose into police business now that he's back in town. She must have seen us digging and couldn't wait to tell him. It won't take that ex P.I. long to figure out for what. He's probably coming after her."

Harry gave out a low, sinister laugh. "Only he don't know where she is, cause you can't get any reception in this part of the woods."

Bax took a long drag from his cigarette and coughed. "What are we gonna do with her?"

"Throw her in the trunk. We'll figure out what to do with her in the morning. Right now, I gotta go home and get some shuteye."

Heather thought the same thing. *Why didn't I get out of here when I had the chance?* She couldn't stop shaking, partly from fear and partly because the temperature had plummeted. But there was no way she was going to spend the night in the trunk of a car.

Glancing from one to the other, she tried to spot a weakness to give her an edge. They didn't appear to have any weapons besides the shovels. She'd have no problem outrunning them, having trained for a marathon last year, before she met Jack Steele and was talked into dropping out.

Bax flicked his cigarette butt to the ground and stomped it out. "Wait a minute. Where's that crazy redhead she's always hanging out with? If one of them is here, the other one has to be too."

Harry grabbed her throat. "Where is she?"

"Home in bed. I told you, I was sleepwalking. I'm here alone."

He squeezed a little tighter. "You have one more chance. And you better tell me the truth this time. Where is she?"

Heather gasped for air. "I. Can't. Breathe."

He loosened his grip. "She's probably close. Call out and say you need her help." He tightened his grip a little. "And make it convincing." Then he took his hand away.

At least she was free of him now. Heather cleared her throat. *I hope my aunt realizes something's wrong.* She edged a little farther away from the man and cupped her hands around the corners of her mouth. "Aunt Julia, can you hear me?"

Bax poked her in the ribs with his shovel handle. "Louder."

Heather doubled over in pain. She drew in a sharp breath, and in a louder voice, she yelled, "It's Heather. I need your help. Can you hear me?"

They waited. No answer.

He poked her again. "Tell her to look for the lantern light. She should be able to see it. It's on extra bright."

Heather grabbed her stomach and gave it another try. "If you can hear me, look for the lantern light."

Only silence prevailed. Heather edged away from the men and kept a vigil in case one of them raised his shovel. But they only waited, glanced around, and listened.

She might as well make the best of the situation. "See, I told you she wasn't here. No one is." Heather got into her start-race position. She was already doubled over from the shovel handle to her ribs.

A shadow moved stealthily behind a tree near Harry. Then it moved again, behind another tree. This time a little closer.

"What's that?" Bax's head bobbed back and forth.

Harry swung around to look.

Julia jumped out with her red hair flying in every direction and her yellow bat raised high above her head. She brought it down with a whoosh, barely missing Harry's shoulder.

He clutched at his heart, staggered back, and dropped to the ground with a thump and a loud groan. He closed his eyes.

Heather grabbed his shovel before he got up again. Bax took off toward the black car.

Julia recoiled. "I didn't even touch the guy! He keeled over when he saw me swing the bat." She dropped it to the ground.

"You probably scared the living daylights out of him."

Julia pressed her hands to her cheeks. "People are dropping like flies. The curse is getting worse."

"You have to stop blaming everything on that curse." Heather felt for a pulse. "I'd better call for an ambulance. He's still alive." She took her cell phone out of the man's back pocket. "Stay here and keep an eye on him. I'll go to the road and make the call."

She couldn't believe she felt sorry for a guy who a few minutes earlier was ready to lock her in a car trunk all night and dispose of her the next morning.

She'd lost her flashlight somewhere in the woods, so she used her cell phone to light the way out. A bright flash came toward her. *That must be Chad.*

She waved. "Over here!"

As the light came closer, it shone in her eyes and blinded her. It was practically in front of her before she realized it was Madam Z.

"I'm glad you're here."

Then she saw the gun.

Chapter 37

Madam Z aimed her pistol at Heather. "Put the shovel down."

Heather dropped it. "I have to get to the road and make a call. Your brother's friend, Harry, has had a heart attack. He might be close to death."

"My brother told me. Take me to him."

"Don't you understand?" Heather waved her arms in a gesture of urgency. "I have to call an ambulance."

"No, you don't. I've known this man for many years. He's one of my regulars. Harry only needs my special elixir to fix him up."

Heather led the way to where her aunt stood over the man.

Julia brought her fists to her hips. "What the heck's going on?"

The madam sized up the situation in a few seconds. "Come here and get him," she called out to no one Heather could see.

Bax came from the road. He grabbed Harry's limp body under the arms and dragged him toward the car.

Madam Z waved the gun at them. "You two follow."

As they walked, Julia leaned into Heather. "We wouldn't be in this mess if the police hadn't confiscated my derringer."

Heather could just imagine. *We'd probably be in a shootout right now.*

As soon as they got to the road, both her and her aunt's cell phones lit up and buzzed.

Heather pulled hers out of her pocket. The madam knocked the phone out of her hand with the gun.

Heather rubbed her fingers. "Ow."

"One more move like that, and I'll shoot you right now." She motioned to Julia with her flashlight. "Drop your phone, and do as I say, or I'll never take the evil curse off you, and I'll tell the police you attempted to murder Harry."

Julia dropped her phone.

"Now open the car door and help my brother slide Harry into the back seat." Julia did as she was told, which was odd. Julia never obeyed an order without question.

"Now get in next to him."

Julia climbed in, which wasn't like her either.

Too bad she left her baseball bat in the woods.

Heather was about to follow her aunt into the back seat, but the madam stopped her with a nudge of her elbow. "You get in the front passenger side. My brother will drive."

Bax got in the driver's side, rolled his window down, and lit a cigarette as he waited for his sister to get in the back seat. After a drag, he flicked ashes out the open window. "Are we going to your studio?"

"Yeah. I have to get some of my special elixir into Harry. He'll be right as rain in a couple of hours. He gets these attacks every once in a while."

Bax glanced at the rear-view mirror. "Then what are we going to do with these two?"

"First, we have to find out what they know. And then a quick-acting poison made from plants that can't be detected. Not like what you did to Esther. That was unbelievably stupid. I had her convinced to hand over the land grant to me."

Bax's shoulder shrugged. "That was Harry's idea. She discovered him following her and said she would expose all of us. He couldn't let our little money-making operation go down the drain. Not after all the years of hard work. That set him off. He never could control his temper."

Heather gave him a wide-eyed glance. *Good thing I have mine under control.*

Bax took a long drag from his cigarette and blew the smoke in Heather's direction. "And he would have gotten away with it if Julia hadn't come along and dug up her body so soon afterward."

Heather rolled her window partially down and sucked in a breath of air. "So, Harry was the evil entity she thought was following her?"

Bax grinned. "A little intimidation so she'd spend more money at my sister's."

Heather's mind worked over this new information. *It was the land grant he was searching for in Esther's apartment. These people are despicable.* She glanced toward the back seat and couldn't help wondering what her aunt thought about all this.

Julia stared at the gun in the madam's hand. Then she gasped. "You'd never have gotten the grant from Esther. She's was ready to sign it over to a prominent land developer."

The madam snickered. "And to think, I wasted months of my time working on the woman."

Julia looked away. "Like you worked on me? I can't believe I trusted you to get rid of the crone's curse. You're nothing but a scam artist."

"I know what I am, and I'm excellent at it. I had you convinced you needed the right herbs, scents, and rituals to rid yourself of this curse, and don't get me wrong, I do believe in curses, but your own power and energy would have rid you of it without help from anyone or anything. You can't imagine how effortless it is to take money from superstitious, gullible people like you."

A moment later, the car turned into the Vendeglo Restaurant parking lot and pulled around the back to park behind the madam's studio.

Madam Z and her brother got out of the car, and she motioned Heather to follow as she aimed the gun at her. "Help my brother take Harry inside."

Bax opened the car door. "Hurry up. I can't do this alone."

Heather sauntered over to him as Julia pushed Harry's limp body out. Then she slammed the door.

Heather waited for her to come out, but she didn't. *What is she up to?*

After a few moments, the madam motioned to her brother. "Get her out of there."

He opened the driver's side door and stuck his head in the car. "Get out of the car!"

"Or you'll do what?" Julia sounded annoyed.

Heather couldn't believe her aunt.

Bax reached into the back seat and grasped Julia's arm. "You'd better do as I say, or my sister will shoot your niece right now."

Julia lumbered out of the car and picked his hand off of her arm. "Your sister's not going to shoot anybody."

Then she planted her two feet in front of the madam and cracked her knuckles.

"Listen, you charlatan, I may be superstitious, and a little gullible at times, but I'm not stupid! I know about guns. I've had several of my own over the years, including a .38 Smith and Wesson revolver like yours, and you can't fool me. That gun's not loaded."

Heather held her breath. *I hope she knows what she's talking about.*

"Yes, it is." The madam sounded adamant.

"Did you check it before you slinked off into the woods?"

No answer.

Julia sneered. "That's what I thought."

Clever, Aunt Julia. Heather let her breath out.

The madam flashed a light on her gun and squinted, trying to get a better look. Then, she handed her brother the flashlight as she flipped open the cylinder to inspect it.

A split-second later, Julia snatched the gun out of the elderly woman's gnarled hands and flipped the cylinder closed. She handed the firearm to Heather. "Hold this while I call for help."

The madam cackled. "Get it away from her, Bax."

He pounced on Heather, seizing her arm, and twisting her wrist to get at it. She held tight. *He's not getting this gun away from me.*

He struck her face. Something warm dripped from her nose. It stunned her for a second, and he was able to wrestle her arm down to shoulder level.

Now he's done it! A streak of red flashed across her eyes.

She grasped the gun in both hands turning in the direction of the restaurant, and squeezed tight.

An ear-piercing shot split the night air, shaking Heather down to her core. Glass shattered, and a million tiny pieces dropped to the ground, setting off a screeching alarm.

"Police are on their way!" Bax grabbed his sister's hand. "Let's get out of here."

The two ran to the car and sped off, leaving Harry on the ground.

Julia gave Heather a tight hug. "Great going. You've got guts." She pulled a tissue from her pocket and wiped Heather's nose.

Heather's entire body vibrated. Her face stung. She stared at the gun in her hand. "I thought you said it wasn't loaded."

"Sorry, I forgot there might still be a bullet in the chamber."

Heather had no come-back for that. Her mind was blank.

A moment later, the parking lot lights came on, and the Vendeglo brothers ran outside to inspect their shattered patio door.

A black and white with its brights flashing and siren blaring, skidded to a stop in the parking lot. Two uniformed police officers jumped out, and one turned the alarm off.

Julia grabbed the gun from Heather and wiped away the fingerprints with her blouse. Then she shoved it into Harry's flaccid hand.

Heather stared at Harry lying on the ground. She could barely breathe. "What happened? Did I kill him?"

"No. You're just a little dazed." Julia rubbed Heather's arms. "We have to get out of here before the police see us."

"But the gun..."

"That's why we have to go. I can't have anything to do with guns right now, or I'll be doing community service in this town for the rest of my life."

Heather gasped. "I see your point. I'm fine now." But her knees wobbled, and she still couldn't wrap her mind around what just occurred.

They headed toward the street where Heather had parked earlier. Chad's car pulled up to the curb behind it. He got out and rushed over to them.

"What happened? I searched the road by the cemetery, but all I found were your phones. Then an alert came on the police ban radio about a break-in at the Vendeglo Restaurant. As I drove here, I saw your car parked there. How did you get here? I thought you were on foot."

Julia waved her hands in a frantic gesture. "It's a long story, but right now we have to leave."

"Why?"

"Don't ask questions. I'll explain later." Julia rushed toward Heather's car.

Heather's knees buckled. "I don't think I can drive. I can barely walk."

"Delayed reaction." Julia said.

Without question, Chad swept Heather up in his arms.

"We'll take my car."

Heather leaned her head against his shoulder and felt the rise and fall of his chest. The steady beat of his heart reassured her everything would be okay.

But everything wasn't. How typical of her aunt to run away from a situation she didn't want to deal with. *She's wrong.*

"Stop! We can't leave, we're witnesses. We were grabbed by the people who killed Esther. And then I shot out the restaurant patio glass door with, what I thought was, an empty gun. And these two men were digging up the forest, searching for a corpse. And there's the cleaner guy lying on the ground over by the gargoyle. They drove off in a black car and left him. You have to call an ambulance. He may still be alive."

"You're not making sense." Chad opened his passenger car door and set her in the front seat.

Julia got in the back. "I'll explain everything when we get home." She slammed the door shut.

Chad headed to the driver's side, but before he got there, the back door opened again, and Detective Lindsey ducked his head in.

"No Julia. You'll *explain everything* now."

Chapter 38

JULIA popped a tiny mint into her mouth. "What are you talking about?" Her demeanor was as calm as if they'd been out for a casual evening drive, while Heather's insides vibrated.

The detective pointed a finger at her. "You forget, I was here earlier, and I warned you about the dangers of being out in these woods late at night. You have a lot of explaining to do, starting with the broken restaurant window."

Julia leaned back in her seat and crossed her arms. "I didn't break it."

"Don't make me crazy, Julia." His pointed finger trembled as he spoke through clenched teeth. "Get out of this car. I'm taking you in for questioning."

She glanced up at him and put one leg out the door. "I'd rather go into the restaurant. The lights are on, and I could use a drink."

The detective raised and eyebrow. "You can have coffee at the station."

Julia leaned toward Heather. "Don't say a word about anything that happened tonight until we've had a chance to talk." Then she got out and slammed the back door.

Chad slipped into the driver's seat and rolled his window down. "You two go ahead. We'll meet you at the station."

Heather put a hand to her forehead. "I'm a little shaky." She rummaged through her pockets for something to eat. *I could use one of Aunt Julia's mints right now.*

Chad lifted Heather's chin and gazed into her eyes, a long, tender gaze. She couldn't help but gaze back with a warm feeling in her heart and a half smile on her lips. *Is he going to kiss me?*

"I know what you need." He reached over her lap, opened the glove box, and pulled out a small white bag.

I guess not.

"This should help."

Heather stuck her hand inside. Her fingers touched a thick, warm, gooey mess. She tried to feel around for something solid, but it was all mush.

She wrinkled her nose. "What's supposed to be in here?"

"Chunks of dark chocolate fudge."

She pulled her hand out, caked with the sweet confection, and licked her thumb. "It's a little messy but still delicious."

Chad's jaw dropped. "Guess I shouldn't have put the bag in the glove compartment and left the car in the hot sun all day."

She tried to suppress a laugh, but she couldn't. Chad's lips curved into a wide smile.

Reaching in the back seat, he picked up a box of tissues and set it on her lap.

"Never mind," Heather said. "I'll just lick my fingers clean."

They both burst out laughing.

***

After a long interrogation at the police station, it was good to be in her own bed at last, even if she didn't get there until five this morning. Although she hadn't set an alarm, the sun shining through the cracks in her window shades woke her. She rolled over and sat up to check the time.

It's almost noon. I should get out of bed. She plopped down again and closed her eyes. "I'm too tired."

The invigorating aroma of coffee brewing filled the air. *Aunt Julia must be up.*

Heather dragged herself out of bed, slipped into her short robe, and sauntered to the kitchen. Her aunt sat on the living room sofa, coffee cup in hand, and surfed the few television stations they could receive with only an antenna.

"I wanted to see if the restaurant alarm going off last night made the local news. It did, along with a bulletin about the police searching for Madam Z and her brother. But they didn't report much else yet."

"Thank goodness. We've had enough publicity."

Heather poured herself a cup of the piping-hot brew, added milk, and took a cautious sip.

Julia clicked off the television. "Do you think the two of them got away?"

"They didn't have much of a head start."

Julia came into the kitchen and set her coffee cup on the counter. "Let's not talk about those people. I talked enough at the station."

"One question. You said you knew the gun wasn't loaded when, in fact, it was."

Julia raised an eyebrow. "It's called bluffing. Haven't you ever played poker?"

"I have. But not for my life. How did you know it would work?"

"First of all, Madam Z could barely hold the gun with her arthritic hands. And second, because I've done it before. Didn't I ever tell you about the horse trainer I once worked for down south?"

"No." Heather settled back on the kitchen stool. *I can't wait to hear this.*

Julia's eyes glazed over as she recalled a, no-doubt un-pleasant, scenario from her past. "Bill was rather attractive, in a rugged sort of way. I fell hard for him. Then I found out he was a thoroughly appalling man. He got me into, and out of, more trouble than I care to remember. But he taught me all about bluffing, how to keep cool when everyone else is panicking, and when the time is right to take a chance."

Heather had to smile at her aunt. *She's known some interesting people. I don't care what my mother says about her, I can learn a lot from Aunt Julia.* "So that's where you picked up the expression, 'Sometimes you have to take a chance.'"

"Exactly."

Julia headed toward her room. "Why don't you make us a couple of omelets and some bacon. I'll go out for the Sunday papers and pick up sweet rolls from the bakery. We'll have ourselves a real Sunday brunch."

***

After they'd eaten, Heather sauntered to her bedroom and dressed. She checked under the bed for the new pair of flats she'd bought.

Meow.

Makki sat scrunched inside the empty shoe box.

"What in the world are you doing here?"

The cat climbed out and stretched his long, sleek, body. Then he scampered over to her and rubbed his face against her outstretched hand, his pink nose sniffing the air.

"I'll bet you came up for some bacon, didn't you?"

Why am I talking to a cat like he understands what I'm saying?

At the word *bacon*, Makki gazed into her eyes.

"Maybe you do know."

Heather slipped into her shoes. "Okay, follow me to the kitchen, and I'll get you some, if there's any left." She picked out a few morsels and placed them on a plate for him to gobble up. Then he gazed up as if to ask, "Do you have more?"

"I'm afraid that's all there is, sweetheart. But the next time I make bacon, I'll be sure to cook an extra piece for you." She picked up the cat and walked to the living room.

Julia sat on the sofa holding the sports section of the local newspaper.

She's probably reading about the Kentucky Derby.

Heather hoped her winnings would be enough to keep things going until she could figure out a way to get her online marketing business started up again and profitable. Or if worse came to worse, get a short-term job in this town. If there was such a thing.

Julia put the paper down. "Where did you find that trouble-maker?"

"Makki was hiding out in my bedroom. He probably came up when he smelled the bacon cooking."

"He's a big cat."

Heather kissed the soft fur on top of his head. "And extremely intelligent."

Makki looked up at her.

Julia took off her walking shoe. "If he's so smart, have him sniff this and then show us where he hid my other red stiletto sandal."

"You can't train cats. He does what he wants. But right now, I'm taking him back to the bookstore. Ashley's probably worried since he's been up here for a while."

"Wait." Julia slipped her shoe back on. "I'll come with you. I want to see if they have books on the occult. If I'm going to rid myself of this curse, I need to know what I'm up against."

Chapter 39

THE minute Heather entered the bookstore, Makki jumped out of her arms and onto a nearby shelf.

Ashley's gaze followed him as she sat in her usual place behind the counter. "Was Mak in your apartment again?"

"He came up for bacon."

Ashley smiled. "I'm not surprised. It's one of his favorites."

Chad came out of the back room. "How are you feeling this morning? I mean this afternoon."

"I'm a little tired." She rubbed her nose and her stomach. "And a little sore."

Julia ambled around the store glancing at the books on the shelves. "Do you have anything on the occult?"

"We have a few on the shelf below where Makki's perched."

Julia took a book down and paged through it as the doorbell tinkled and Detective Lindsey sauntered in. He greeted everyone and leaned his thick body against the front counter.

Chad strolled up to him. "Any news, Benny?"

"There is. Harry woke up this morning. He'd had a severe attack of angina, but he'll live. The physicians at the hospital are baffled about what Madam Z gave him to keep the man going. He should've been under a doctor's care."

Julia lowered the book she held. "The madam has an extensive herb and flower garden on the side of her building, along with a thin volume explaining the secret knowledge of plants, trees, and herbs. It's probably where she gets the recipes for her magic elixirs. By the way, did you catch her and her brother yet?"

"No. But they won't get far. Harry confessed everything."

"I don't blame him." Heather said. "They ran off and left the poor man for dead. Did he tell you what they were digging for in the woods?"

"The murder weapon."

That's the last thing I'd have guessed. "What was it?"

"A wooden mallet. The gardeners at the park use it to drive plant food stakes into the ground around the trees."

"I would have thrown it in the lagoon," Chad said.

"Harry admitted he panicked when the police car rolled into the park, so he took it to the woods. Then Bax reminded him families camped there in the summer, and the school kids with their nature hikes. He couldn't take the chance of someone finding it."

"Have you discovered whose body was burned in the warehouse fire yet?" Chad asked.

The detective walked to where Julia stood with her open book. "Harry told us it was Madam Z's husband. He'd been living in Mexico under an alias. Came back for money. She poisoned him with an elixir. Then she tried to make it look like he was killed in the fire, setting Julia up to take the fall."

Julia shook her head as if she was shaking off the whole incident. "I still can't believe it." She closed her book. "Well, detective, it sounds like you have everything wrapped up."

Lindsey scrunched his aging gray eyes. "Not quite."

"What do you mean?" Julia tilted her head.

"Since no one was home upstairs, I came here looking for you."

Meow.

Everyone's gaze turned to Makki who had settled himself on top of the tallest bookshelf and was batting at an object.

Plonk!

The red stiletto fell to the floor, landing at Lindsey's feet. He bent over, lifted it with his index finger, and then dangled it in front of Julia's widening eyes.

Heather suppressed a laugh. "Gee, Aunt Julia, when you told me you felt like something troublesome was hanging over your head ready to drop at the most inopportune moment, I didn't think you meant it literally."

Lindsey's lips flattened. "You swore to me you didn't know the whereabouts of Krystal's other red stiletto."

"In my defense, I'm as surprised to see the shoe as you. The only explanation I have is that Makki stole it."

"You're blaming it on the cat?" Detective Lindsey put a hand to his lips, covering a mocking grin.

Julia's fear-filled gaze darted around the room. "No. I'm blaming it on the crone's curse."

Heather could only shake her head. *Why Not? She's blamed everything else on it.*

Epilogue

JULIA sat forward on the living room sofa hovering over several open books spread across the cocktail table. She ran her finger down one of the pages. "*Sky Magic.* I think this is it!"

Heather climbed off the kitchen stool where she'd spent the last hour in front of her laptop, and grabbed a donut from the counter. "Haven't you made up your mind which ritual you want to perform yet? It's been a week." She had given up trying to convince her aunt there was no such thing as a curse and was now embracing the madness.

Julia looked up. "With Madam Z in custody, I'm working off the top of my head. "We're lucky Lindsey convinced Krystal not to press charges and no more bad things have happened. But even my luck can't hold out for long against the evil power of the curse. It's just a matter of time."

A knock at the door startled Heather.

"Who could that be at nine o'clock on a Saturday night?" Julia sounded annoyed.

I hope it's Chad asking me out on a last-minute date. Please... But just in case it's not... Heather put the donut down, went to her purse, and grabbed the pepper spray. She made her way to the door. "Who is it?"

"Me."

That voice. It couldn't be. She sucked in a breath, opened the door a crack, and peeked out into the well-lit stairway.

Jack Steel leaned against the door jamb dressed in a navy blazer over his white dress shirt, and designer jeans. His thin lips curved into a half-smile.

Heather's shoulders dropped. She let her breath out in one big whoosh as her heart sank to the floor. Then she slipped her finger over the pepper-spray trigger.

"Aunt Julia, you were right about it just being a matter of time before something bad happened."

The End

Thank you for reading, *The Crone's Curse*, the second book in the Willows Bend Cozy Mystery Series. If you enjoyed it, please leave a review. Reviews are extremely important to authors and also to readers like you, so why not take five minutes to leave a review on Amazon today? It really does make a difference.

Other Novels by Evelyn Cullet:

The Charlotte Ross Mysteries:

Love, Lies, and Murder

Masterpiece of Murder

Once Upon a Crime

The Tarkington Treasure

The Willows Bend Cozy Mysteries:

You Bet Your Life: Book 1

An *Author Shout* Silver Award Winner

A Dance with the Dead: Book 3, coming this fall.

For more information about her novels, check out Evelyn's website: https://evelyncullet.com/

About the Author

Evelyn Cullet has been an author since high school when she began writing short stories. She wrote her first novel while attending college later in life, and while working in the offices of a major soft drink company. Now, with early retirement, she finally has the chance to do what she loves best—write full time. As a life-long mystery buff, she was a former member of the Agatha Christie Society and is a current member of the National Chapter of Sisters In Crime. When she's not writing mysteries, reading them, or reviewing them, she hosts other authors and their work on her blog, **https://evelyncullet.com/blog.** She also plays the piano, is an amateur lapidary, and an organic gardener.

Made in United States
Orlando, FL
02 March 2022

15318280R00128